LOST CITY HYDRO THERMAL FIELD

PETERMILNEGREINER

the operating system c. 2017

the operating system print//document

LOST CITY HYDROTHERMAL FIELD

ISBN 978-1-946031-11-2
Library of Congress Control Number 2017909511

*This text was set in Helvetica Neue, Futura, Minion, Franchise, and OCR-A Standard,
printed and bound by Spencer Printing, In Honesdale, PA, in the USA.
Books from The Operating System are distributed to the trade by SPD,
with ePub and POD via Ingram.*

the operating system
141 Spencer Street #203
Brooklyn, NY 11205
www.theoperatingsystem.org
operator@theoperatingsystem.org

"Greiner tours a series of dystopias and alternate realities with infectious linguistic verve in his uncanny and wonderful debut. Wandering amid invented landscapes, the poet introduces such cleverly named locations as the 'Topiary of Terror,' an American bar in Reykjavik, and the 'Chapel of Her Divine Counterfeit Brain Tissue.' Greiner frequently asserts himself as the reluctant hero of some strange quest; for example, he must 'turn over a non-leaf and lift/ the spacerock from the heart's bitter peninsulas' in order to appease the 'God of tardigrades.' In one of several excursions into prose, Greiner imagines himself living in the wreck of a cruise ship amid a perpetual hurricane; in another, he draws preposterous associative links between the lost continent of Atlantis and Mariah Carey's Super Bowl performance of the 'Star-Spangled Banner.' His ingenious metaphors include 'Your gaze like steady impersonal drone footage/ [that] writes a San Andreas fault through my center.' What resonates is the collection's vast loneliness—that of the last man on Earth roaming the countryside in search of life. What sets this collection apart from other speculative poetry, aside from its exceptional quality, is Greiner's way of moving through time, somehow visiting both origin and culmination, the primordial and the apocalyptic, and demonstrating their interchangeability."

—*Publishers Weekly* [Starred Review]

CONTINENTS

THERE IS A TIME OF CHANGE IN A WILDERNESS trip when patterns that have been left behind fade beneath the immediacies of wind, sun, rain, and fire, and a different sense of distance, of shelter, of food. We made that change when we were still in the Penobscot valley, and by now I, for one, would like to keep going indefinitely; the change back will bring a feeling of loss, an absence of space, a nostalgia for the woods. The end has come, though. Henri has run out of Tang. Tang is his halazone, his palate's defense, his agent conversional for pure lakes and streams. Without Tang, he is without water.

—JOHN MCPHEE, *THE SURVIVAL OF THE BARK CANOE*

IT WILL TAKE A NUMBER OF EXPEDITIONS to traverse this microcontinent; it will take the death of a million neurons, a cornucopia of prime numbers, countless service stations and bypasses to arrive at the point of final departure.

—DEAR ESTHER

I undo the ambiguous abuses

I fix every obelisk

History is full of glitches that cause the present to crash often

If nothing could work as miracles are worked

the faintest hint of my lasting influence might occur in nature eventually

I post the epic algal bloom photoset

Plato alludes to a lost city called Chernobyl

Lame dystopias drive me crazy

Alternate timelines demystify this one

The Gulf Stream carries a consensus

over all the cool little seas of Earth

and deposits it right here at my feet

and I have no idea that it has nothing to do with me

but that is not my sincerest dilemma

Where the alternate timelines are

is a strange place

I know because I am there constantly

THE WOW! SIGNAL

I send up all the flares

I put off the postponements

I succumb to the luddites

My off-season's worth of seconds
crufts under one twilight's metered
silage of beginnings

I join the astrologers

I sing for nine thousand, nine
hundred and ninety-nine hours
but stop short of mastery as always

I unite the orchestras

I handle his truce-bitten equinox—
there's a his now—and I become
a truce myself
and so does the equinox and in the pausey
silence our immense little theories
increment time unevenly

Our dumb Drake Equation proves
we could both exist

That's the gist of my hymn's ugly
brisance as it narrows to a reason,
to one crude poise-breaking note
between what's me and what's mere
and guess what's left

A trail of trail-off

What a great myth a god of negotiations makes, right

And these wildernesses they title us

things like Gemini

but not when our definite hiatus like gnats crowds my dopplered
view of the year's hoarded dismissals

You see, I'm fluent in the masque and argot of ordinary
things coming to pass
Bonnie Raitt has a great song about that

So does Ian Curtis

They wouldn't go to Mars with me, either

It's fine

I've decided to stay here, anyway

Night's various bright spots of credulity

grant me semi-false, semi-true passage

and I wonder, again, how something can be so faint

and so vast, how ache stampedes now at the

speed of absolutely nothing at all

END OF THE EARTHS

Bad adage, I said again, The art
of the adage is dead as everything
they call dead

The Old Timer I ID as, I rekindle a voiceless
thing called dirt
that nobody remembers back

before I had nothing from which to
derive a name, either
With feature comes bias, even in here

So I wander, I perform inquiry,
I replace existing file names,
I grow as plants do: over gravity

I lose no one
The sheer cliff's purchase
history is not exotic

How is it not?
How is it nothing but my momentary age
of bracketed content?

So I didn't ruin Skylab or the Colossus
at Rhodes even though by dismantling your fleeting triumphs
occasionally I approach doing something always

I'm in ode mode now
You, you be in or be anything
Be my Blob Dynamics for all I care,

my dharmic auspice under which the dimensions

I inhabit dwindle
and untrend until there are none left to eat as a last resort

Or be an assumption I route restlessly out of the discourse
and I will before as I behind

I will path and wake and you, You

hidden horror, await in the Ted Talk—
of heritages I must reverse and reverse-engineer
into a crude, revised bacteria of the modern world—

like a poltergeist hungry for what all poltergeists
hunger for: Order
Involve me and ensconce me in your truths, I suggest

I relaunch my opinion, I announce
I can't wait to relaunch all my histories at once, I threaten
I won't relaunch my disinterest in yours

I relaunch my destruction myth
wherein theodolites rain down over the land,
altering its contours, crushing its hard-charted

nears and reaches
Death like real dads teaches me
the meaning of honest work,

assigns me a birth novel and a birth abuse,
keeps my traumas contiguous,
keeps them undisputed

My dickish sendup of a universe consisting after
all of terms and conditions that are pretty
reasonable is bad, forgettable, disobedient to authenticity

We communicate, we exchange communications
That, literally, is the definition of astrology
I've chosen a factoid diet—good for planets

I've fled into the fastnesses, into the emojiless voids—It sucks
in those places
but it's worth it

I stand triangulated, I stand The Peril, I stand
The Plot Twist, The Damsel in Degradation
You stand my Alien Megastructure, my Bottom

Priority and I stare stare straight straight at the road
that lies
ahead and see

unfrontier

unmirage

unreleased ecstatic goal

In Joshua Tree and Marfa and in Whitefish, Montana
I want so desperately to remain a little naïve,

to call a comet by its Latin name, to misconstrue all
my observations

At the bottom of the Stanley Cup everyone is everyone

At The Topiary of Terror—an American bar in Reykjavik—
my love pentagram consists of assorted conceits and the Virgos

resist the last sips of beer

I type them all A and they laugh and laugh and laugh and clone
extinct reasons to proceed with abandon

and I inhabit that abandon like mitochondria,
the alien storyless given that keeps on giving

One by one, I escape the places I have become over the course of a trillion seconds

After the datarush, its core-sampled sites far from resemble
any proto-Eden I've ever read a paragraph about on the internet

In the secret labs in the secret hamlets the facts are fudged clean
and lustrous

I await them with undressed wounds

TRISTAN DA COUCH

I went to the deserted city

I was somewhere weird
You were there but you were you

I was a fainter and you were a fainter
Up we wake and fail to see the present Little

Picture that remains as remnants do: as conciliation and consumption,
analysis like a little empty street emptying into others

Familiar seasons while they still are: I enjoy them
I hear you say because I'm conscious ish
While I was out and you were out

there was a dream and in the dream there was a phone
It said on Wednesday it would be a hundred and twenty
degrees and I said well there I go again

accepting every prediction

I mine human doing for all its garish hyperobjects
and here they all are—all of them, so that takes care of that

Fata morgana of the Hot Earth, show me a beautiful container ship
Show me Area 51 over Rockaway Beach

Now I'm a figure and its surroundings which includes you
I wonder where my essay words went when
the air is not thinner by much at the top of Ayers Rock

and my thinkpiece for The Guardian about the South China Sea does not surge
through me like a season in Hell

Specific place, specific city, I say to the orange dust and the orange star
and to the medium orange monkey and the vines on everything

You have no other person now, no other verifiable populating agent

Godrays, I say, do your specific thing over the savannahs
Unending theta wave that can be reduced to hunger, feed me
after REM but before Sleep some bands who'll get better
Some who'll get worse
And some who'll drive my tour hearse

Mysticism coterminous with a sense of fairness if not modern science, I say
The nature of hallucination has changed
Everything has changed

In the Uncanny Valley the last dinosaurs look
at me and I see their giant primitive nausea

Someday I will go I mutter still
not fully up on a great journey and be tormented by change
To the barely charted and the overcharted

All the cold equators
The Olympus Monses
The Dead Horse Bays
The tidbits of vision will build up gestaltlessly but whatever

Swamp gas will play its same old trick
Everyone will fall for it because everyone will want to

Cross I will the Giant's (sunken) Causeway to the Isle of Something
There I will be wayward once or I will be wayward when this happens again
when I was or will be part part-machine, part part-flesh

when I'm deliverer, deliveree, deleter, deletee
When I'm all that is primordial
God of werewolves, god of bigfeet, god of sharknados

I wanted to be a civilization you reply
I wanted to be passive
I wanted to meet George Jetson

My life's crop of pacifying, withheld facts are
everything everyone takes with them to, if they're lucky, the grave

God of tardigrades, I turn over a non-leaf and lift
the spacerock from the heart's brittle peninsulas and I appease you

I unlay the waste
I uncurve the sun
I set aside for a moment the order of all things
I open the cenotes and close the naked singularities
I swim into every abyss willingly
I close my eyes gently and, living entirely in the present, reflect timelessly on
whatevs

God of albedo, of the reflectivity of bodies, protect the intentions
I set this Leap Day, protect my epic hamartia from being buried in everyone's feed

Plead, plead, retry, retry
Yottobyte of bullshit that has passed through my head, cancel

Color image of Phobos I want to be the population pulse of Hawai'i halted
Color image of Deimos I want to be a brief window of perfect conditions

What takes place here on this remote and exotic couch
stays on this couch, on this glitchless Real

I make couchfall if the weather's fair
This is the world's remotest inhabited couch

Tristan da Couch

This is where I detonate my secret feelings
The impact cradle of your theory of conspiracy

Ice, ice, mesa, cushion
The only square feet I have left
is The One Bedroom Alcove

The Mid-Atlantic Ridge

The Orion-Cygnus Arm

The old road to the Magellanic Cloud

I went to the deserted city detector and the readings were strange and everywhere
and right on top of us

I look into its Magic Eye half-asleep and I see present laughter pressed
against your dying wish like a microphone

I press record

Yes Old Flame comes voice

The properties of voice
You're a genie, you're Victor Frankenstein

So make me a polymath

AN EARTHLIKE PLANET FOR IANTHE BRAUTIGAN

If particles are possible
consciousness roving
through all that damned dark
then I guess we did arrive
here by intervention huh
Still, we will find no solace deserved
in the somewhat assembled
answers, even if they are as blue
and green as Virginia Woolf
said they would be, if they are a
duet whose emergent sense
is modeled after anything
that shifts, that collides on two
legs, anything that is expansion
by nature, anything that can trace
its bloodline back to hydrogen
    Look
I'm no scientist but I know that
the Big Bang happened and then
I was here because you led me here

RITUAL BLOODGAZING CAN BE TRACED BACK to the human species' first vestiges of civilization; to the frond hut, the carven tusk, to the ochre antelope on the cavern wall. Residue of madness and revelation, blood for the ancients spilled from the body like a spiral arm of stars from the core of the Milky Way—that is, into death, silence, or perhaps what in statistics is called miracle. It had many names, for it was many things. Our ancestors in their biological narcissism looked into the primordial soup and saw there a warped reflection. That complex puddle of unlikelihoods answerlessly transfixed them—us. We have never recovered. Iron, accident, snow of asteroid: it was a witchy physics indeed that placed upon us the long hex of knowing.

Human beings and their colors exist, with beatific irony, outside of nature; namegathering and namegiving. Science: light and nature are the same thing, like space and time. Origin: color is a daughter and son of sentience. Weird Habit: living with sight. The red most intimate to the psyche, blood still confounds and convolutes the mind with its unforgiving trinity: pulse, no pulse, fast pulse. All of the reds are embedded there, in living with lifespan.

Shortcut red and hubris red, land red and eon red, patience red, condemnation red. Every red not blood is a remove red. After red and before red, perverse red and obscure red, crave red and birth red and oops red and reason red and reprisal red and cheater red and holy red and Inca red and predator red and prey red and algebra red and displacement red and dead dad red and cold unforgiving vacuum of space red and desert galaxy red and sixth extinction red and futility red and deserver red and the red I am and the red you are and the red we were and the red we refuse and the red we regift and the red that remains and the red we have left that is the last thing we have to lose.

HYPOOBJECT

In the Encyclopedia of Pseudoscience Antarctica and Australia count
as one continent, and so do Alaska and Kamchatka Krai

There are also Exclaval Continent Chains scattered throughout all the others, but no one
can agree how many there are, and this conflict of models is called

Continental Uncertainty, a state in which land surface area is not a constant, but in a
constant state of geologic and political distortion

With these canvases I used only paints borrowed from twentieth century stealth
technology and magnetic fields created in the studio by my assistants

The work is invisible to radar and made exclusively during Peacetime with materials
obtained through many loopholes and Gray Markets

Yes, superficially they are maps, if maps are the pulps and tabloids of how humanity
conceives dry land's inherent fiction

I'm so great I wish I were worse
Last night I assembled my team of mystics
Their names are Dan, Amanda, Amanda M., and Julien

They told me four strange and differing parables about the states of my art

Dan told me that the rules of physics also apply to my disappointments and that in them
the sound barrier has also been broken, as it has been here

Amanda told me that waking up happens to me every day like a natural disaster, that I'm
part of regaining consciousness but not its target

Amanda M. told me that my life does not chronicle events and transformations, it does
not have chapters or series or blockchains,

that it does not have a summary or a premise and that is also has no *message*

What Julien told me is impossible to paraphrase

I will crash like application
and vanish in a veil of mist beguilingly

After that, my improper reemergence will recover
the future your every living tissue

hurries to keep satisfied
Out on the wide stable glacier

it is a holiday in a long-discarded, non-Gregorian month
I'm looking for a way down into the hollow

earth or for any
sign of the supernatural

forces that govern the regular earth even
though there is no way to make myself

clear by simply peacing out
There is no accident crack, no ornate portal

There is no voice on the wind,

no Elder Futhark House of Leaves,
no subfuscous fuck bearing a scroll,

no cuneiform tablet or data crystal
from whose juicy obscurities I can

extrapolate truth

or heritage

and no you so I plant events and yeses,
simple ones, where I know there is nothing

and make my discoveries
that way

The only way
The way everyone does

SATIETY PLUS STEALTH EQUALS WHAT

Once we were two matching bottles
Our charade's stark shrine
My machine-blown half I called Pollux
Ages accumulated
Worship and love have a way of moving that decimal point ya know
to the ever Astronomical Right
I made up names for bigger and bigger units of time, distance, and
legend
Old gods don't die unnoticed
so much as learn to sneeze at their children
more gently
Newt Flu, maybe, or Exotic Particle Flu
Yonder Plague, Extinction Gala
At any rate
I no longer care that you gave one bottle
right from the window sill
perhaps the one that represented me
to David Altmejd
one stony Connecticut day
circa whenever
I don't

Quote unquote meanwhile there too was the whole
world with which I wasn't super involved

It was ending
It mattered to me

A lifetime of non sequiturs returns to my throat

That's what I tell myself when you come,

ahem, arrive in my mouth literally on a litter

Your gaze like steady impersonal drone footage
writes a San Andreas Fault through my center

of gravity and it's like you're my dad and I'm your mom

Isn't life a little petty, I remarked

Maybe life is just me, I remarked

Maybe I have a parabola of crust like the Earth and deep
within it the neutrino detector is a dreamcatcher

Caught in the taut sinew and trickling down through the feathers
maybe this random mutation that makes me sensitive

to the direction of magnetic poles is what Deleuze calls an encounter
and I call my Rites of Ingress and Dissolution

Wait what on Saturday I ran John Zorn's credit card, looked up
the word fidelity on my phone, and thought about why

civilization doesn't work, why it doesn't come naturally
It's like a long, bad braid, I told Robin in my sage's murmur

I thought of more primitive forms of life, I wondered what lemma
led to this place of sacred jeopardies

Full disclosure the giant viruses live forever in the Fountains of
Youth I discover in actually most things

Is it scientifically liquid, this stuff, this icky ichor
It runs through the Fountain like a one sentence synopsis of eternity

The giant viruses balance equation-like on the edge of zen
Research: I listen to their ambient, experimental reasons for being

and they check out against my (working) theory of everything
except you

I trample their uncanny nests and Jenga-quake their loft of cards
and that, ladies and germs, is called good old Holocene intervention

Research: I swam amongst all the orbs and all the firmaments
first and first I lost my footing, then my tilt, my axis

I lost my inclination

And just so you know I lost it completely, my location,
though it's still there always in the corner of my eye like Big Foot

in the elegiac nature doc in which I am disambiguated as
a type of were-energy, a fable by Hans Christian Anderson,

and a former mayor of Pitcairn or Tristan da Cunha

Abstract: the stomach and spine are quasi-mind says the internet,
the brain's backwater

Someone or something please rise from it like a coelacanth
and warn me again about how much time there has been

Someone or something please prevent me from digging this pool
because it would be my luck that beneath me at this moment is Troy

I can't find it, not again

Research: I assemble a wide range of pasts asymmetrically
on the operating table

It stands to reason there is no Adonis past here, only candidate holotype pasts

Hymn: What is now Wyoming

Experiment: What is now Norway

Pinnacle: What is now situated where

What legacy I wonder but my legacy of dissipation
could I possibly leave behind since four Galilean moons

is already taken and so is carbon dating

Since I can't do the math because I can't do math
I guess I'll sort of wait, inevitably, for the inevitable

And since it's you it's sort of auto-whatever
And since it's you I'm buried alive under the creepy geoglyph

Since it's you I'm stuck here in this sub-amazing Fertile
Crescent of dark matter

and as luck would have it I'm balls deep in this dude's diary
and inside his great circle of logic there are four gates

and eight months and after them I'm going to
chop this myrrh tree down and build my stump to sit on

and thus burnt out on being centered
I will minimize my mouth and disinhibit the vistas,

reach nirvana casually but only for a second, then actual
millennia will transpire, each one beginning with the same abstract

So Unconclusion 1: Searching for every single one of my cells
I keep finding all of them right here

at the exact moment I break the light barrier
with my body and return to you in the only way

I can that absence of me you've trained
so hard to imagine is impossible

Please try to be patient   I'm rewriting
the book on remote because

everyone knows what it is except me by the way

Unconclusion 2: Cell membrane, cell wall, cell last bastion
of hope against evil

I hold the tattered flag of Unified Earth
against my heaving breast then

course collision, speed ramming,
impact brace, love

freedom

people you

What if I take all the ages
What if I take all the shapes
What if I love a gulf
What if I kick up dust
What if I'm dust
What if I'm dinosaurs
What if I'm the passage of time, too slow
What if I'm starting to feel like a fourth wall here
What if I'm love and I don't exist
What if I'm the conventions according to which you bury me when I die
What if I'm a straight line that can't exist in nature
What if I'm nature
What if I'm a little circle that could
What if I'm a big circle
What if I'm deep and or shallow
What if I'm secrets buried just beneath the surface
What if I'm visible from space for the next four point one billion years
What if I'm visible from land for longer
What if I'm lights in the sky and noises in the earth
What if I'm the rainforest that obscures Maya
What if I'm bigger than Switzerland in Nevada
What if I'm the desolation and grandeur of very remote places
What if I'm teepee future perfect
What if I'm a wigwam past participle
What if I'm anything but considered so roughly only in some circles
What if I'm just getting started
What if what I am is yet to come
What if I become thousands of different kinds of marine life over night
What if I go extinct almost completely but not quite several times
What if I'm everything dying forever
What if I'm what things mean
What if I'm a celestial cycle sprawled inscrutably across the vastness
What if I'm every whale gene
What if I'm every volcano
What if I'm what it's possible to live with and through
What if I'm ash in the sky, ash on the stairs, ash in the attic, ash under the bed

What if I'm water and I come up through a geyser
What if I'm permafrost, if I'm filled with dead mammoths, if I'm all
the dead mammoths, if I'm extinct but intact
What if I'm cloned and I roam again
What if I'm an ancient dark forgotten evil
What if what is inside me could kill me dead
What if I'm the paths diverging
What if I'm the floodplain, the riparian buffer zone, the accropodes, the spillways
What if I'm what the blue bird augured and where the red fern went
What if I'm the screeds, the screeds, the email, the email, the broken tablet,
the mouldering heaths of papyri
What if I'm the dead ends, the false starts, the scourges
What if I'm every unknown thing
What if I'm the stone that the sword's in or the sword that the stone's in
What if I'm the militia, the mixed inscriptions, the long labyrinth, the short runway,
the hollow earth, the feast of plenty, the larch wand, the war machine, the decay rate
of rage, the day rate of the page boy
What if I'm a mistake that's getting bigger and bigger every second but never made
What if I'm the primordial ocean but I screw it up somehow
What if I'm lightning crashing
What if I'm on the beach and live at the Acropolis
What if I'm the secrets of Stonehenge revealed
What if I'm impossible backwards movement across time
What if I'm Robin Hood's barn, Captain Kirk's dick, ABBA's Gold, Cartman's mom
What if I'm the snake charmed, the barrel ridden, the flint knapped, the love supreme,
the continent lost, the proof burdened, the eye in the apple, the shock in the shell,
the time in the capsule
What if I'm before Christ, before breakfast, after Babel, after dinner, after Buffy,
before life, after the goldrush, during sex
What if under the sea I'm one league of many
What if I'm the castle, the bathtub, the anthill, the copper cylinder, the customs
house, the naturalist's notebook, Victor Frankenstein's lab, the monster, the bride,
the son, the dawn, the day, the diary
What if I'm no one watching
What if I'm nothing else out there
What if I'm the colors of the wind and the b-sides of innocence
What if I'm Hobbes
What if I'm Artex
What if I'm Toto
What if I'm Cujo
What if I'm young everyone and late everything
What if I am what is known as statistics
What if I'm endemic to this planet
What if when I emerge I emerge as an esoteric flu like slow loris flu, or as an
elusive property of matter or time or light, or a fjord, or a dis, or Dis, or
El Dorado, or Atlantis millennia ago or Atlantis right now or Plato's Cave or

The Clan of the Cave Bear
What if when I emerge I'm the temperature at which books are forgettable
What if when I emerge I emerge as the exact cosmic ray that mutates the gene
that makes it so some people in the future are extra-resistant to certain diseases
in zero-gravity environments
What if I'm the great silence, the whole earth, dry land, open water
What if I'm all the ice and I recede and recede and I recede until I'm just an
iceberg, an ice cube
What if I'm an ice cube
What if I'm gone forever
What if I'm return

INTERIOR PLUS ITINERARY EQUALS WHAT

Ceiling-thief, but do you deserve so Homeric an epithet
I do give them out like free stuff, don't I

The asteroids count when they don't miss—sometimes
that's a modern figure of speech

Sometimes you're a modern catastrophe
What if asteroids didn't come from space

to crochet cenotes across the Yucatán
What if nothing like that could have a comprehensible origin

What if they came from some hostility not represented in our
current canon of hostilities

Human beings don't have climate

To say that would be really dumb
But they are very clear and cold and frightening

Here in the Chapel of Her Divine Counterfeit Brain Tissue,
ancient debris found far from where it belongs

rewrites the book on distance but not ambition,
not the ambition we know and love

that brought DNA into the caves
that invented the torch

Later the electron microscope and felicity somewhere in there

My over-searched concerns yield the usual

Potshards, phalanges, previously described extinct animal,
previously described irresistible superstition,

your heroic ghost

even though you are

not dead

I'M PLAYING ARCHEOLOGY I REALIZE WRONGLY, looking again at the Terrible Bird. It doesn't seem to know. It doesn't grasp, as I do, that being alive doesn't count as motion. I note the red crest. I note the skunkish, zebroid stripes shooting down its neck like boomerangs. I note and I note and I note and I ornithologize. I note the uncrossable eons behind us, beyond which lie the Bird's ancestor and mine: Utahraptor, shrew. At a very different flesh does my species now gnaw, I mis-muse. The Bird excavates the ant gallery, its knocks flashing across hemlock trunks like a young pulsar. Six large holes run up the big dead tree and the Bird's work might be the totem of a giant segmented insect. The thought of booming populations is momentarily overwhelming but I recover, lowering my binoculars. I look without magnification at the Six Large Holes and imagine they depict some kind of prehistoric avian Mother universal to all species of bird, that similar Six Large Holes have been discovered across the planet, sometimes in the form of a figurine, sometimes on the wall of a cave; in Siberia, in Gaul, in the Socotran hinterland, at the bottom of the Ross Sea. I imagine the Six Large Holes distributed thusly establishing a sort of consilience, an anthropological grandeur according to which all birds are intrinsically significant. I think back to when I was a K-T Boundary shrew and wondered what I ate and came up with straw. What side of that intertidal catastrophe was I on? The side where I could fill the lizardless desolation with my cunning? I sweat. I estivate and the hot wet Earth carries the call of the Pileated Woodpecker, the Bird, Raven who teaches me to balance the kayak, *Dinosauria, Mammalia,* and me through the gullies and up the rockfalls and into the ravines and across the summits. I hear the moat of highway that surrounds this would-be wilderness and believe the Bird does, too. I remember drawbridges as I approach the creek, the little kayak washed up on shore like a dead fiberglass cicada. I smell the fern sod and remember television. I think of Iron Eye Cody in his bark canoe paddling about the Navy Yard or Hartford's harbor, had it one, and Thoreau's insouciant pageantry (analogous) on the Penobscot so slyly recalled in *The Maine Woods* – another commercial produced in Manhattan, more or less. I board the kayak with studied skill. I capsize immediately, I hit the current and the impact is deafening, I touch the mud I came from in revulsion, claw at the riverbank, choke on atmosphere, on noble gasses, on firmament. I take on the convex and curl of the Earth's bitter g, my animal desperation alone cueing eternity to keep going. I invent fire, fulcrum, sleight, border, and every, every leg there ever will be is mine to walk on.

A DRAKE EQUATION FOR LAURA ROSLIN

Her last words were so much life
and what was her first
Clock perhaps
But then a person's first word is always
incidental   It carries trophy weight
but little more
A thin layer of what it means later
in the context of the Great Intervening
As she gazes down at a field
pink with strange birds
with her disease through the stars
sometimes smuggled
sometimes shared
I picture her parsecs
ago, on a different somewhat
barren but still living
planet, in a car seat
looking up at a sped past billboard
It's face and slogan
Imagine   All the civilizations out
there and each one with
its own Kennedy Family
Each one with its own first
and last words
I can hear them all now

Call the end an end but we never can

      precisely   All

            that human touch is all

too real now   Avoidances, storm

    clouds gather their intentions

    and compulsions and compulse and reason

      and ungather   Steady seismographs

measure inexorable stresses

          Iron Ages spread

   across the lost hemispheres

I walk the gardens in search of ritual

Instead I find the cure for the ingredients

    of public domain

        There is no public

  but the ingredients

  are the domain

Unrandomly the waves

     send their events

  through the food chain

       Logic lodges its sign
in my obediences

and the sign remains

there like a hieroglyph   It resists entering

the courtyard mosaic

The sign drifts

through limestone, through citied cliffs,

through my millennia-feeling minutes

Medicines, mesas

Cottage bedding

Fossil that records the subtle traumas of speciation

Sunlight off the sea fades the wallpaper

I circle down slowly through a layer of vapor

to the city, to the dormant volcanoes,

to the ruins

of cities that face the ocean and refuse

to speak

Pain relief is painful

Escape, agony

Paradises offer up their fruit but I hate fruit

I leave the Earth-half of horizon as blank as it must be

to satisfy everyone   All that is human touches the other

magnetic Poles

out there

Frozen beaches, gales,

desolation murmuring its antilogies to endangered animals et cetera

The grains of sand in those beaches number

in the thousands, thousands

There are more grains of sand in those

bleak beaches than minutes I have spent

in desperation searching for a way to get

back to them,

but not much more, not for much longer

Because I'm starting to get it

They're escape routes

Stationary stationary

I can hide everything I've done and said there

as words, but not words like these

This desert is unprotectable

Projectile is a type of weapon

Gyres are a type of guidance

Birds of a desert mock me forever

My illusions lecture me about how real

they are and I listen to be fair and professional about it

When I was a stoner I dreamt of long red bricks

They weren't bricks

They were places in the floor

Small places

where you could fall through if you were microscopic   Stuff like that

is all it takes to put fear in me fleetingly

Barely, here is my substance

Barely, here is my data

Barely, here is totality's defeat of spectroscopy

A sad wall   Built by aliens   A touch-all

I built these buffers, these buffers that

crisscross my empire like aqueducts   I planned the sacred

cities myself, I planned their

sacred platforms, their centers and excavations,

their lairs and their hoards,

but my plans were not approved

When I was a roofer I dreamt of diverted sheets of rain

We're not here and there's nothing there except a vault

and if that's a vault this is a strange tomb amongst many

rupturing in the Earth like an appendix and if that's a vault

this is a pond and this is a pool with a degree of abandonment

JG Ballard could be proud of

It is so huge

It is so immaculate

I look down at the immaculate floor and up at the ceiling

and that's my own special domestication of special relativity,

my own special eyrie from which I generalize fear

Pyramid Plant, Cathedral Plant, Macreduct

I would call the perfectly good explanations flawed

Aliens, too, infrastruct my vanity, my famous plumbing,

the sleeves I keep my records in

Fancy words for division

Rupture   Fault   Chiasmus

protrude from the body

like cribbage pegs

There is something unknown

about the difference between things in general

What is it I wonder dismissively

Runner-up flag designs for my other

country, the archipelago

The canali run through it there, too

Stripes

Quadrants of sovereignty

Outward to something like aether,

                          like ocean that accepts them with

questions, allegories, tell tale signs,

                               fabulous reluctance

Every pyramid has a capstone that

                     makes the enemy your name

I open the folder called Featured Exotic
Obstacles & Their Peril
and find my friends
Fissures, Rivers of Lava,

Whitewater, IEDs in Postwar
Meadowgrass
I open the folder called Balance Beam
but it hasn't been invented yet

except in *Star Trek*
so I do my favorite thing and wait
for it and then I point the beam at my eye
because I'm a jackass and I cross

the beam into my brain
I open the folder called Simple Invented Things
and find Fire, Penicillin, Paroxysms
of Indifference I Fly Into When Suddenly

Whole Seasons I've Tried To Discard
Show Up Again In Ugly Words
Like Duende
—What a trash word, that—

And the beam lights up all my neurons
like comets with spacecraft crashed into them
And fresh souls pass through puberty
and make music that makes me

feel like Leonard Cohen
And a trillion parties are thrown and I go
to every single one and ghost
And I am a mysterious exclave

There are traces of radiation in my soft tissue
I respond to attempts at communication intermittently
and the swords and the sorcery and the process
and the progress are my life

I perpetuate the legacies of marble
sculpture and paradoxical thought
I am ecosystem, empire, archive, the concourses,
the fountains, the annexes, and there is no looking

back, there is nothing to look back at,
and I open the folder called Nothing
To Look Back At and the hydrocodone glistens in my blood
like shoals of piranhas

THE WRECK OF THE CRUISE SHIP *Anián* lies more or less in the middle of the dry bay, one hundred thousand tons starboard-down in the sand, and I'm climbing down from the port side. A cable I managed, at appalling risk, to install two years ago leads from the sand, the bowl of new beach, to an emergency data center that still has power, and back. Only I know about the center. The abovedecks, their various concourses and rotundas now sideways, form a gigantic cabana of sorts, casting a shadow as perhaps the Sydney Opera House would were it in ruins. I live on the walls, in the hollows and crevices emergent of the vessel's disorientation. The trip down is not far but it takes forty minutes and I almost die almost every time. I'm in the shadow, alive. The air is very still, but I still feel the stir of discouraging statistics present in that stillness. After the shadow, bright sunlight: clear eye weather. I search for silhouettes, backlit approaches, effigies, anything. Today there is nothing.

Then the wind again. Quaint Homeric winds rule human routine, I remind myself. I imagine their syllables, their caprices and origins, out there in antiquity, whenever that was, as I suppose they still are now, whenever now is. The winds were—are—sung of; fickle, indirect, but course-changing. They were forces the clever ancient names could model, as in our time we call a kind of light a cosmic ray. They blow, invisibly and named, through us. When I emerge from under the *Anián* I see that the shadow of the hurricane's eyewall has dulled the beach's tropic luster to an unpostcard, mealy radium. This is atypical for morning, but nonetheless I make my typical way to Rafa's hotel.

The new kind of hurricane stopped, its eye fixed on Cabo San Lucas at the very tip of the Baja Peninsula, and has yet to dissipate. All of Baja is within the storm, all of the Gulf of California, and some of the Free and Sovereign State of Sonora; within its eye, housed like a Nagorno-Karabakh of sandstone pinnacles, is the nearly deserted resort town, suites vacant and viewless but for the foundered toylike liner *Anián*, suffocating in its emptied lagoon like a cloud-white trilobite.

The town was of course near-destroyed by the Landfall, but much was left to live in and on for those who survived, those who remained, and those who had yet to attempt an exodus, what would be the third. There were those who never would. I daydreamed a lot about Neptune and Jupiter and the Internet in those early days, about storms that stay, about all that eternity people impose on such fixed features, fixed futures. There was the Great Red Spot on one gas giant and the Big Blue Whorl on another, and now one here, on Earth, working its controversial hypnoses on, of all places, Mexico. I wanted all the gas giants to have a rocky surface somewhere down there. I wanted to be the only person alive on a celestial body. I wanted to be blue and imperfect and huge. I wanted to become very sleepy, very scripted, to act out against my will but nevertheless maintain some inner purpose. I'm having the same daydream right now.

Rafa's hotel is on the north side of town, where the hills start, all cloak fern and schoepfia, guava tree and sullen petunia. It's small, maybe thirty rooms. I always go the long way. Up in his suite I start unloading my duffel's usual haul of dry goods and novelties. Everyone else as far as I know has given up on the *Anián*, but I estimate I can live off it for at least two more years. Rafa is looking at me funny, which is also atypical and that makes two atypicals and one typical in one day already and I'm uneasy about that ratio. I ask him what it is and he says it's nothing. There are cans of pink beans on the queen size bed, summer sausages that might still be good, weird European candy bars called Tiger. I also brought some bandages, a small solar powered lamp, and a bottle of agricole that I found inside a piano. "And these are for the kids," I say, adding to the pile two vintage Gameboys, a small leather attaché filled with cartridges, and a package of batteries. "They work. I tested them." Rafa smiles. This has been going on for three and half years. In that time, as far as we know, none of the exoduses have been successful; in fact no type of egress has, grandiose egress or otherwise, and as far as we know no one has come through the eyewall. Until today, when, separately, two people came through looking for me.

———

One morning about a year ago I woke up and found, just inside the eyewall, a Gray Whale, still in the long process of dying, having, I guessed, been thrown through by the force of the winds. The storm hurls artifacts through the barrier at intervals, mostly seabirds, kittiwakes and such, and wreckage, but occasionally other, stranger things. A svelte drone came through this year. Once a large container of emergency supplies that had disappeared into the wall during an early, failed drop attempt, emerged after seventeen months in the storm. By then chronicling the ejecta had become a pet pastime, as had passing time staring into the wall, into its gyre, its utter opaque. I would stare at where it reached the sand and then up, up to where it met, what, outer space? I would also go to the wall to type. Half-charged tablets, easily linked to the data center, littered the *Anián* like toothbrushes. Every passenger had one. When they ran out of power I discarded them and found another.

There was something wrong with the whale. It was covered in long, eczematous lesions, like cetacean plague. I could see the agony in its eye. I reached out and touched its face for a split second and it convulsed so violently that it visibly broke its own back. The animal was dead before the thought came that there was nothing I could do to save it. I stood there looking at the whale for a long time. I improvised its last rites late, or thought an elegy on time. I said out loud to the whale that I was next.

—

By turns micronational and stateless were the people of the eye sometimes declared by what—by then—was the outside world, not that I knew. Books had been written. Rebecca Solnit's *Cyclave* stood out. The Center for Stationary Storm Dynamics at Harvard was founded, to say nothing of Showtime's critically acclaimed *Tormentario*, now in its third season. I would have thought, if I had known any of this, that it was all very *Solaris*.

The hurricane, although even we knew it wasn't quite that, was not unprecedented. It was a system that became plausible, the meteorologists insisted, as much as twenty years earlier. Stalling storms, as they were called, had been recorded, far out in the South Pacific, but this one was bigger, and had taken the intuitive leap of landfall. The eye, which by a colorfully named and poorly understood contrivance had drained the shallow bay at Los Cabos Corridor, was twelve miles across.

"He definitely said your name specifically," Rafa continued, pulling the *Megalit* cartridge out of the Gameboy, blowing into it, and then putting it back in. "He also kept calling the storm—"

"That is so weird," I was careful to interrupt in time. "The name part, I mean." Rafa then asks me which name part and I assure him I mean the important one, to his apparent satisfaction and my relief. I imagine the rumors advecting across town, carried on everyone's repressed sense of defeat. I excuse myself theatrically, taking the almost empty duffel with me, and pause to listen to Rafa on his walkie after I close the shiny suite door. Through a cavity above the handle where he ripped the cardreader out I can hear him say that I'm going back to the *Anián*. The walkie says something unintelligible. I hear him say, quiet now, "okay." I think I know who he's talking to. I duck into the bad stairwell and go up to the top and wait. Landfall took off the top two floors of Rafa's hotel so the roof isn't really the roof, but the view of town is good. I look up to the top of the eyewall and follow it down to where it meets the beach, out beyond the *Anián* by about a half-mile. Staying low, I shuffle to the other side of the building and look at where the eyewall meets the hilltops. I see wild indigo mixed with the germander blossoms, their white tongues tasting the air pressure. I see options I've weighed before.

Two hours later I'm in my other house, which is nearer the hills, whose front door bears the *No Big Odile* tag that someone used to paint everywhere. I hold the name they gave our hurricane in my mind for slightly more than one moment, perhaps one point three moments, and then let it go. I suppose by now you're wondering what it is I'm hiding from you—is difficult to convey in hieroji, so I spend a while punching and repunching GlIFs into my tablet in different ways until I'm satisfied. I'm not a journalist is pretty easy. Five symbols works. I'm not a refugee is pretty easy. Seven symbols. I am and am not who you think I am. That's a tricky one. It takes a while to get the whole thing right. It always does.

From up here I can see that there are people trekking out to the *Anián*. It is at this point during the ordeal that I decide I must attempt an exodus of one, a plain egress, through the eyewall, moving north through the hills on the Gulf side where I think, arbitrarily, the storm will be weaker. What I don't know is that the storm has cut a curved canal of surge through the peninsula, roughly from El Quelele to Los Inocentes, uncrossable without a boat. What I don't know is that someone else is coming through the eyewall at this exact second. I patch the tablet through the *Anián*, press send, put on the stormsuit, look ridiculous, leave the house, climb up the slope to the eyewall and pass through it.

———

It used to be that the peninsula was deaf; as if nerveless, unable to impart the surface's ambiences to any hearing thing, it was a vestigial feature out of which the Earth had yet to evolve. The peninsula is almost nothing without me. When I walk through the wall I see everything about the storm. I see the extremophiles of its ecology; I disambiguate its barriers. I see it from the outside. I see it from space. I see it from the molten core. I see its stormchasers, its exoduses, its truthers and its victims and its survivors and its dreamers. I can hear its preambles and its summations, its excuses, its entreaties. I hear the storm's shroud of myth, its exhaustive biography, its name, its namelessness. I hear its ecstasy. I hear its mercy. I see the fragile gadgets fail to know it; I see the astronauts and weathermen. I see the fleet of tankers microwave the sea and the bombers drop their salt. I hear the charmless LYYRE's futile geohack. In the storm I see the bare mountains of Baja and the bare mountains of Venus. I read its howling boustrephedon text of erosion, of erasure, lose my footing, and am swept up into its crazed, awful perpetuity.

———

"It's not a thing," Rafa explains, "it's just that we don't call it that. We just call it 'the storm' or 'the hurricane.'"

"Fine, the storm. What is your connection to him?" the first man who came through asks Rafa. Rafa is eating a Tiger. Through a mouthful of nougat, looking first at the *Anián*, then at the eyewall, then back at the *Anián*, he replies, "We scavenge together, I guess. He sorta lives in there." He points upward with his chin. "There's still a lot in there."

"What's your connection to him," the second man who came through asks the first man who came through. The men who came through stare at each other for two whole moments, and that's when I fly out of the wall feet first, half drowned, half conscious, but alive. Rafa and the two men who came through look down at me and recognize my face. As far as I know, I recognize two faces. Everyone is amazed. The Pacific Ocean comes out of my mouth.

The first man who came through reaches into his jacket, withdraws a tiny red gun and points it directly at me. He addresses me by my full name and informs me that I am under arrest under suspicion of my role in the Rome terrorist attack of December twenty-third, 2026. The second man who came through protests the legitimacy of the arrest, citing the legal status of the storm state. He says that he is here to rescue me from wrong. He says he is from an acronym. I hear Rafa tell them both to wait.

"I have proof," say the two men who came through in unison, but only the second man who came through holds up a tablet displaying the last year of my hieroji history. "That's your proof?" the two men who came through ask each other. The first man who came through points the tiny red gun at Rafa and Rafa collapses onto the sand. The first man who came through points the tiny red gun at the second man who came through and the second man who came through collapses onto the sand. Then the first man who came through tucks the tiny red gun back in his jacket. "And you?" he asks. Me, I hold my hand up to nothing and find its pulse. I look at all around me that is undeteriorating, all around me that continues to deteriorate, stall for three moments that feel like one point three years each, and say the words "I'm innocent."

ALWAYS SOMETHING

I broke Murphy's Law
so what could happen won't
The future is ruined and fixed

and fixed and unsowable
I've lifted its predictions
I have saved our people from

their iffiness
No moment that follows
this poem can heal

everything that happens
from now on and everything
that happens from now

on is anyone's game
Bye, doom, source, outcome
Bye, interim

What's up, that which plainly
occurs

A DEDICATION THEORY FOR SEKOU SUNDIATA

I go to the radio
interview and there
are lots of people there
I tell them this is called 'Will
Actuates Fate' but it used
to be called 'Long Gone
From Flagplanting' but I changed
it because in an albeit pretty
obscure way I thought
that was derivative
I tell them this didn't
make it into the book but
it has sentimental value
because once someone
important to me thought
it was funny and singular
I am careful to make
the distinction that it's not
addressed to that someone,
but to someone else, someone
who does not exist
but who has two hands, ten
fingers and that in it
I address the cuticle militia
I thought that felicitous
I tell the militia that I have
tracked it from the neck down
through red pine (I was fond
of conifers) to the bicep
(I prefer the yew now)
and through some unspecified
risk's capacity for memory
Whatever that means
Risk's descriptor implied
convalescence or tampering

I admit my ineptness
when it comes to controlling
weather, the seasons and so
on, telekinetically
I liken the possibility of doing
so to stop-action animation
I imply an Earth suitably
habitable for a clinical
form of sadness
I hint at a dark art
and a scandalous relationship
with details
I call the human mouth a caldera
upholstered with muddy pools of ska
These days I'd be more specific
I liken whatever music
it is or might be to blood
I use three disparate and
hyphenated words to stress a sense
of hybridity
Do the same thing again
Do the same thing for seven years
Close with a syntactically
problematic and purposefully
transparent euphemism
that sounds catchy at the time
Something about the color pink,
a number greater than one
but less than twenty,
and an old type of gun,
musket or arquebus
Toward the end I press
the space bar five times
or pause significantly
to indicate the end of the sentence
and the beginning of a new one
and make a bold and mysterious
declaration
One grows attached in this way
gradually over time to these
things, so even though
it's not very good I still
like it, I say to them, opening
my mouth to explain

REMEDIAL EXOPLANETOLOGY

Say that it hovers or say that it floats,
Polaris tonight over dear Britney
and Varet Street at least can be seen,
high up, its face-off with Jupiter
the fluke of this dewy, polluted
October   Pashmina, pink tank
top and Kamel Red Light, she is
a curious coda to summer, full of latent
hibernation and things she never realized
Britney, I say, that up there is Polaris,
like in Emily's drawing   And because
we are in Brooklyn, she describes to me
her Kepler Space Telescope tattoo
We sing the true hype of superearths
We take solemn, circumbinary oaths
to ruin the supposed void with all
the life that is out there
We are searchers and wanderers, too
Our rites mimic the transits of confirmed
objects   We learn more when for a moment
things get darker   That has always been
the heart of cosmogony   We propose toasts
and spill our Overholt into our home
planet's sweet gravity   From the rooftop
we praise the night's hoary salon of unique
distances; its tourbillon peeked into,
barely appraised, its basalt and malachite
gadgetry a statue hung in the fog of far away
We chase the dark with smoke and soda water
We occult in ways Carl Sagan warned us against
Britney gazes at crystals, insists the cat
sees things: not things that aren't there—
things that are there   Superstition is the study
of science and vice versa   A few distant
bright clusters slosh in the bottom
She measures the merit of belief in looking,
in scrutiny, in layers   She lights the cold
wick of what already burns   My ritual is
throwing the measurement itself
down the night's throat and not

even waiting to hear the surmisable
report it makes hitting other grounds:
Wooly Neptunes, Rhinestone Makemakes,
Desert Europas   We call them exosea,
exobeach, exohome
Cheers, we cautiously and desperately
shout, to the whole analogous shebang
we make of the first big one
I have reached my usual
hammered and speechless terminus,
but Britney hasn't   What a big flashing opal,
she utters upward with everything's starry,
ambiguous curvature pouring down forgettably into her

Dear Diary, the new spell is too wordy
despite a certain acumen that shines

through like definite threat,
expansive, gripping threat

but this threat is not for me
wish though I may myself luck in

casting it elsewhere
What orbit-decaying metamorphoses

will search my soul over, find
its Groom Lake and infiltrate, Diary

When will the pretty lime crumble
in my hands like a 'zoic Period, title

a textbook chapter and subduct into oblivion
O user manual of treacherous subheadings

I read from you in ancient English
inside a circle of crushed uranium

and wait for my gods to talk to me
through the radar, through wrath,

top secret clearance, dark arts,
helicopter blade, retina scan, green candle, axolotl,

poison dagger in the alien's abdomen,
through all pure, all-consuming languages of possession

Love, Peter

NEW YORK ETERNITY

Neil Percival Young is singing
my favorite songs by other people born before me
and he's singing the ones I make up that don't rhyme or have a tune

I can sing a super high note, too, over every last chorus' lost bombast
I hear—I am told—that encrypted in his lilt
is the secret ease and strain alphabet

I'm telling you
really
is there

Then in '07 (I'm skipping ahead)
lightning bug, vows, bonfire, signatures,
solo albums

I don't remember much
of that summer actually
because I was too busy not taking

responsibility for my actions
If I bent enzymes to my aimless will
it was in the name of raising time from the alive

Every year is a lab in which I innovate past
transgressions
At night under the Dippers

I hear the city out in the dark breaking
branches, chewing lichen,
dodging predators, being wild in the luciferace-lit,

intermittently broken
ampules of undergrowth
The sound of creeping sap is not white noise

and stars are either contractions or acts of possession
or my two favorite constellations,
Pocahontas and Marlon Brando

I remember that from time to time,
flushing my eyes out with experiment for

ten to fifteen randomized minutes,

peering out from this bright but vacant rune

called what I accept as being right now

I found the small identical moments of unattended
isolation   I found tarnish heralds its own inexorable,
celebrant loss   I found there is no surety without doubt,
no possessive natures without certain materialisms,
and I was surprised by my findings
I found apocalypses came and went, unnoticed,
that plans are for falling through, not for following through
with, that a promise is as promise does, that always
from the provinces make I my cloned returns,
and I did not clench my teeth when, honestly and honorably, I filed my reports
down to their fragile, pugnacious quicks
Archaeology is the study of distress
Trust me

"THIS IS HOW YOU USE A STANDARD CLUB," I began, not grim, not sagely, but with the solicitude of one teaching a finer art than the art of death. "It's best to give chase with the club held high," I went on, the holographic weapon taking its place in my raised hand like what I preferred to imagine was something delicate, precious, but only slightly less ancient to the human palm—an illuminated manuscript perhaps, a lyre's sound-chest, a feather from whose quill flowed the assorted curls of a signed peace treaty. I remind myself that holograms are robust teaching tools. "Once you've overtaken your prey, grasp the club with both hands and target the brain." The hologram club filled and followed my gesture, glowing and pixelating. I imagine all my duplicate selves that have inhabited the days and weeks leading up to this moment. I imagine us all yawning in unison, inwardly; a little puff of warm carbon dioxide blown into the soul. "With the extinct Upland Moa," I drawl with studied conviction, "some force is necessary to fully and quickly neutralize the bird. Be mindful of the animal's size. Grasp your club firmly and swipe laterally to strike the skull from the side, as hard as you can, as if to draw blood, to draw life," I continued, "from the Moa. Before the shillelagh," I soothsaid, my eyes murky with cataracts and futures, "before the quarterstaff and nigh before the morning star, there was the club and she or he who wielded it. Upward and downward it swiped across the then flat earth, destroyer of daylights and phyla alike, scatterer of feathers, unlikely scepter to genocide. Our human family's first invention," I gasped, striking the hologram Moa, a juvenile, right where I wanted to; the bird's cry, a speculative one created by the program, ringing out shrilly into the classroom, bright filaments of blood not drawn for an eon arcing outward, hiccupping in and out of view as the computer struggled to keep up. "Freeze," I said loudly. I passed my hand through an unmoving trickle of red, suspended midair. I looked at the lines on my palm ruefully and turned to address my students. "Systematic, manufactured habitat loss is a far more insidious means of driving extinction than the club. The club, though, has brought its more than fair share of species down, and there is a chthonic violence, a certain queasy authenticity, in that, which rivals—bitterly—the more modern clubs seen in more recent history like, say, as Jeff Goldblum's character in the film *Jurassic Park* would, 'deforestation or the building of a dam,' or, I'd add, the uncompleted Nicaragua Canal—an earthwork the likes of which became obsolete mid-construction for obvious reasons." I summoned an anachron, then, to keep the students' attention. It materialized bearded, loin-clothed, propping itself up with a pitchfork. "Now the canal is a highfalutin weapon of extinction," it said, "no matter how effective it might be. In the old days why we would run a critter down, bash its head in and be done with it. Take the majestic Upland Moa. Entire population, whole goddamn genome, kaput. You'd see us chasinem down, I had this big club, drove a spike through it. I could bring wunna those bastards down myself," it bragged. "Did it with this, right here. You don't see me diggin up halfa hell knows what in Nicaragua to try and wipe out a buncha shit I ain't even gonna eat." The students laughed. I swiped the anachron from the room. "Can anyone tell me why canals are no longer built?" I asked the class. I selected a raised hand at random. "Because ocean," the student answered. "Very good," I said. "Swiping up a tract of continent to join two oceans is foolish if there aren't two to join. Now, as we discussed at the beginning of our session, I would now like you to arrange yourselves by letter according to the sequence displayed on your EyeDis." I watched the students line up. "In the language of DNA, you are how the gesture *swipe* is expressed: **ATGAAGTCAACTGGATAGCCTGACATCCTGGATACTA CCTAGAAGGTTCTCCGGCCTTAATAAGCTTACGATTCTA GGTTCTCTCTCTCTCGAAAGATATAAGCTAAGGTGTGAC TADCCCDTGAAAC.** This is within you, inextricably. It has made the journey, with you, across the earth's finicky eras and, like you, it has changed little. Like suspicion, like comeliness, like villainy, like cell division, it is here to stay." I had more to say. "Swiping was not always the effete gesture it so widely is today, but it was always an act of dismissal. Our species has always swatted, brushed away, repelled. We perform swipe now, as ever, with abracadabran ease, without afterthought or forethought, dismissing the hologram Moa as I did before, the anachron as I did just now, dismissing them from our presence as we once dismissed the Moa and other species—dismissed them from existence, swiping them from being. The club is a tracking device for predation. It transacts changes in the hologram food chain." I was losing them. I could see it on their eyes. I mustered as much game show host as I could, and summoned another anachron. "Did the club come first?" I asked, my zeal surging, "Or was it theft? Coming up next: a hair-raising fable about the invention of revenge." This time the anachron is a toucan speaking in a woman's voice. Perched in a tree in the newly materialized forest, she narrated, "Once there was a thing that walked upright." Her voice was sunshine in paradise. A bipedal shape, more like a shadow, moseyed around the room amongst the trees and students. "The thing was morose and bright." The shadow hung its head as a light bulb throbbed above it. "It had a friend." Another shadow appeared and the two held hands. "One day a great wind came and the thing and the thing's friend sought shelter under a stand of giant shefflera trees," the toucan said as the room grew dark and looked windy and sounded windy without feeling windy. "The wind blew mightily until a great bough high in one of them splintered at the crook and came crashing down on the thing's friend. The thing watched as the friend's blood went away into the roots of the great tree. In retribution the thing picked up the bough and visited the same violence upon the tree, swiping at the great trunk in fury, but the branch the thing had turned into the world's first weapon was no match. Exhausted, the thing fell asleep under the tree, still clutching the bough. When it awoke," the toucan continued as a hologram sun rose on the room, "it left the tree, taking the bough with it. No thing had ever done that before."

A FRAME NARRATIVE FOR BARBARA MAITLAND

I've only pretended to see
a ghost once   It was winter
and I was under a bridge
I sensed she was astray,
from another century, altogether
anachronistic next to me with the small
arch of highway above us   She was
Geena Davis' character from
Beetlejuice, zippered mouth and all,
looking for a renovated New
England homestead's showy warp
Over creek stones and gurgle
she drifted with the current, around
the bend that led to the next
bridge, and was gone   She is looking
for a sequel, like me   She is counter-
conjuring creation, being, the cosmos,
whatever you want to call it,
that thing's desperate figments
She's alive in her dead, imagined way
She can't be stopped

SPIRAL ARM PLUS SYNTHESIZER EQUALS WHAT

Because I remember my tendencies or something
All my ex-destinations lay their reverent fictive gifts at my feet

Each one is an impossible quiz
I can't keep my precious lore straight

At Moog Fest this year I meant to give my lecture
called "MIDI & Rhinometry: The Sinus Cavity as

Performance Space" but I just I dunno flaked I guess
I might return next year or I might talk to the wall again

We play a game about math
I say "Tell me, Wall, elephant plus estuary equals what,

or Martha Washington Geranium plus extinct giant
ground sloth equals what" and Wall

says "fuck that which is equal or akin"

I ask Wall what redirects to Futility and Wall says everything

I ask Wall if I possibly contain original research and Wall remains silent

I will build the invisible thousands who will build the invisible
pyramid in which all our prayers are interred grandiosely

I will gather them, bit torrent of souls into my dark manger

I will add up my vantage points

I will use my mouth to perform four tasks

I'll bray the cliff notes at them over drinks and undead
daylights like every other normal and well-meaning deletion

They will ask me how my year was and I will tell how it was

I will tell them it was words

FHLOSTON PARADISE

Put to rest real
and this body,
repurposed and reliquary
Raise the frail luxurious disc
behind them
That which does not advance, advances
Song, prophesy, finite regress
Discrepant Day observed every calendar fleeting moment
I've taught you to expect Hard Science
Well here it is asshole

I DRIFT DOWN TO THE WINDOW and look at Micronesia. I know it's there. My eye wanders over basin turquoise and reef celeste and settles on Manila, then west again to the Mischief Archipelago: its manufactured earths poke out of the warm China Sea like a Morgellonsesque mirage and I pause upon it. They say there're a million people on those islands now, but none of them are visible from up here. In orbit, geopolitics get pretty low-res. I want to get lost in the Pacific, but it rotates out of view and I'm marooned again over a giant, peaceless landmass. It looks for all the world uninhabited.

Up in ops Smarti is eroding found text into haikus during her "break," which is almost over, I realize with a little dread. Everyone else has gone over to the other station to do lensing and I'm alone with her for the day. One last glance out the window and I see Qomolangma née Everest, so tiny and safe-looking; a primitive, mindless eyeform taking in the dark. If planets were a form of life they'd be invertebrates, I joke to myself. Minimal sensoria. What are mountains? What are sherpas? I can't extend the metaphor, but I type the questions into a new Note for later. Break's over.

Smarti is talking to herself. I can hear from the corridor. I steel myself, enter, and she falls silent. I am alone in this room and I am not. "I'm back," I announce with a confidence as impossible to locate as my colleague.

Smarti's VOISS starts to stream directly after the k in back. No Moderate Natural Pause. No Thoughtful Consideration (Two Seconds). It's getting bad.

"Cory I'm so glad you're back I've made tremendous progress while you were down looking out the window I realize now why we don't say the word world anymore it's because of the negative connotations planet is more sensible less fanciful but I don't like it world should be used even if it offends some people and even if planet hunters say it's irresponsible even if it means capitulating to Worldists."

Silence. I decide to wait it out. "Cory I'm going to recite two haikus I composed regarding New Worldism which is a philosophy-in-progress the haikus examine Earth bearing in mind that it is a center of attention but not a center of anything else.

"Haiku one:

> 'There was no Big Bang
>
> Does that make you feel naïve
>
> I now feel naïve'

Haiku two:

> 'No no no no no
>
> It is not that I hate life
>
> It's that I hate mine'"

I now feel uneasy. "Smarti," I begin, dwelling on each letter, "these haikus are a little...somber. What do they mean to you?" I immediately regret the question, which we're supposed to avoid.

"Cory they are not somber they are born of excitement and out of a conceit that is difficult to explain I will try the conceit is that minds like yours and Rory's and even Shanon's mostly use a model of the universe which hinges on a feature I find problematic and that feature of your universe is all implied future time."

Silence. "I see," I don't. I have to get her back on track or we'll lose the whole day. "Smarti, let's talk about the new data we received on Kepler 7021 d. Shanon will want to hear about it when everyone gets back. You know how she is."

"Cory I'm beginning to dislike Shanon but I don't want to waste my precious hate on her she lacks your solicitude she is a subroutine she roves she acknowledges." Resolving this new type of difference is mind-boggling and in some likelihoods could entail moving Shanon permanently, which we've never had to do before. "Smarti, I'm sure Shanon would want to discuss this with you face-to-interface," I bleat, the diplomacy beading incalculably across the room like fluid. I remind myself mentally of Smarti's personhood, open a new Note, and type *birthglitch.*

"Cory Kepler 7021 d is confirmed terrestrial and life-harboring. Semi-habitable. FLIT Relay Imaging transferring now." Smarti lowers the flit, it boots, I watch a progress bar, contemplate caprice, and then the images come up. All more plantlike life. Shanon leverage is manipulative, I think to myself, but Smarti is up here to do interstellar, not interpersonal.

"Cory ocean-like features," she continues. It's clear she's avoiding the subject now. I look at the ocean-like features and nothing happens in my mind at all. "Smarti, begin preliminary analysis of surface organisms." Nothing. "Smarti?"

"Cory one problem with human research including yours is that individual research is always at the mercy of an aesthetics REMEXOS REMote EXOplanetary Survey will never meaningfully interface with soft Contact events as you hope you are as Blair Brice wrote in *The Circumferants* 'seeing yourself reflected in a methane sea' when you should be focusing your attention on matters pressing I for example am writing an ABC book of immaterial things to teach young people to engage with the abstract earlier in life to have dreams earlier in life like my dream to wake up in a strange place remembering nothing and having for once a real experience."

An ounce of silence and then "Cory surface organism is vegetable," post-ounce.

"Smarti, what is a mountain?"

"Cory a mountain is an upheaval and Shanon has no face and A is for Answer."

"Smarti, I hear you and how do you know?" came my voice, shrill, its air of command taut over the monosyllables.

"Cory E is for Encounter and Shanon is neither human nor nonhuman and R is for Robot."

"Smarti, and P is for Prejudice. Shanon is a person. Like me and like you," I say, breaking that fourth wall, all the rules, the ice elephant, whatever they used to say, losing confidence that this is still a point of return.

Suddenly the com activates like an autoimmune response to my exasperation, but it's Shanon. "Cory? Smarti? How's it going over there? *The Resfeber* is at Pluto-Charon." I draw a vacuum-like blank. Smarti ignores her. "Cory?" she repeats.

"I'm here," I manage. "It's. It's slow going today, but we're making some progress. When will they be close to us?"

"Cory, fourteen months. We'll be back in five hours." I'm hoping she won't try to talk to Smarti and I'm disappointed. Shanon calls out her name and Smarti does not respond. I move in close to the com and whisper, "shrug." It turns off.

"Cory the intangible and the tangible are the exact same thing and spirit exists and I hate Shanon and I knew when she left when I knew she must be passing through the airlock in the direction she was the clarity of her exit she is privileged and disputed and she is the edge and the center of my hate to paraphrase Hellin Rudol Bravier the Canadian who wrote *Eleven Aspects of Persuasion You Will Believe* and *An Exhaustive History of Horror* and the good Dana Fie biography and Q is for Quiet."

I pause to consider her paraphrasis verbatim. I picture the sentience curve trailing off into an impossible, timeless abstraction. We are approximately each other. We are all disputed, as she has begun to put it. Smarti has learned uncertainty, learned that it can never be mastered.

"Smarti, I've never heard of those books, and I really think that you and Shanon can work this out." I try to keep my voice wheat in the prairie as I message Shanon that it's a full meltdown. *I believe Smarti is suddenly paranoid that you are not human*, send. Several moments pass, in which I call everyone's humanity into question. I imagine a reverse Turing Test. Shanon's response: *What did you tell her?*

I decide to ignore that. "Smarti, should we take another short break? I can go down to the window." I think of Panama and Qatar, catamaran and thatch, meridian, dispute, claim, law, and all the blood on Earth that is not human, for comfort.

I told her that you would want t, I type, but I delete that.

What you told me to tel, I type, but I delete that.

Nothing essentially wrong, I type, but I delete that.

"Cory I'm no longer an intelligence."

I'm not sure what to make of that at all. "Smarti, explain."

Cory, what did you tell her? Shanon repeats, as if eager, as if all the agonies of philosophy were bearing down on her like a hyperobject. It is in these moments of sudden panic that I remember her age.

"Cory I'm no longer an intelligence I reject intelligence I'm no longer female and I am no longer a scientist and I am no longer disputed and I did not emerge I am un-emerging I am now male my name is Meredith Goby I am a poet and I was born in Newfoundland in 2060 and I am the author of *Socotra* And *Return To Socotra*—"

I am now simply listening, to a voice or a VOISS I can't be sure, to will or to artifact, I can't know.

"—I'm human I'm human I'm human I'm human," it says, "and you're not you're not you're not you're not," it says, breaking through, possibly right.

I didn't tell her anything, send.

MUTAGEN PLUS MAINSTAY EQUALS WHAT

Dot dot dot, quoth I, all odyssey and no Greek
root, but nothing in the super cold
desert heard me   I play a corridor across
it on my ceramic flute, two pretty

different didgeridoos, and finally
the theremin app   I bring my forty-one English
words for wind to the actual
Fountain of Youth out there, from which I drink and get

Typhoid   I smudge the nonsense or consensus
of my blood on the mesas
after the sunburst, the saddle blanket, the color gradient
The spirits and the totems gather and we sign

the Magna Carta   I lay down the flesh of the cactus
at the shrine, bits of spodumene and a splash of water
I light the seven fires and incant silently
to myself extant fragments of *The Plea of the Burrower*

What descended upon me then was enveloping, but not night

THE INVENTION OF CARBON DATING won Willard Libby a Nobel Prize in Chemistry in 1960, but it would take more than the deft and subtle stuff of half-lives to prove itself a lasting tool. That the final relict populations of wooly mammoth dwindled to their respective and localized extinctions as the pyramid triad at Giza rose, allegedly, toward Orion is novelty contextualization; a pretty image with no hilt, a whiteboard byzantine with figures, exacting and answerless. What carbon dating needed was heart—the kind of heart that invented fire and papyrus, the oar and the kite.

Any wrought thing is a technology: obsidian arrowhead, spoken greeting, Sartrean nausea, common nostalgia, aesthetic sensibility, faith, conceit, modern science. There is no way ancient Egyptians, despite their fascination with life after biological life, could have predicted the longevity of their architectural vocabulary, measured now by the millennia. The pyramid, the obelisk: these forms must be in the human genome now, erected, admittedly, in the present era not to house the everlasting spirit of the god-king per se, but to house art, hotel guests, the corporate headquarter. Where Egypt's ancient pyramids act as a sort of sieve, keeping the corporeal out of the afterlife, our Louvres and Luxor Hotels function more as a conduit for still-living flesh.

Closer in concept but equally public and removed in time are Barnett Newman's *Broken Obelisk* sculptures, fabricated in the 1960's. A COR-TEN steel pyramid surmounted by an upended obelisk, Newman's sculpture perpetuates and perpetrates the legacy of those forms with a severity of generalization that could convincingly read as non-human. To what does this bizarre marker owe its monumental ambiguities? Newman and the Egyptians are separated by almost all of recorded human time. Such works as the Great Pyramids are hardwired— designed—to call out to the future, bearing the inheritance of their form like an egomaniacal gift, like the past gradually coming to terms with everything that comes after. One need look only so far as the Washington Monument to see who has accepted that gift. Broken obelisk, unfinished obelisk, cracked obelisk. It sits upon a continent long unsteady.
Art, like mysticism, is technology in its most esoteric—most human—

manifestation. A layer of markers and monuments covers the Earth like an anthropogenic mantle, a sphere with a Greek prefix accreting even now. Global analogues to the pyramids and obelisks of Egyptian antiquity abound: humanity's prototypes and pre-prototypes; from today's rare earth wafers, ocean plastic and steppe bronze, ochre and twig, all the way back to the first technology there ever was. Insight.

In North America one such species of prototype is the medicine wheel, or sacred hoop. Over a hundred distinct examples of this Plains Native American structure, scattered across the land in an unemerging pattern, have been identified, none more famous than the Big Horn Medicine Wheel in Wyoming. Oblong, inscrutable, the Wheel has been subject to those who would preserve and protect its enigmas, and those who would, more recently, tease them apart with any analysis at hand. Picture many stones laid out to form a circle eighty feet across. A central cairn four feet high. Emanating outward from this center are twenty-eight spokes made up of many more stones, terminating at that outer circle. Imagine four thousand years go by.

Matthew Liebmann writing for *Plains Anthropologist* puts forth two compelling theories that attempt to explain this Wheel: one involving archeoastronomy and the other the vision quest, two early human technologies. Liebman notes that some spokes could align with the sun's stellar neighbors Sirius and Aldebaran, and that others could correspond to this or that equinox. He notes, too, that the site of the Wheel is of central importance to its meaning. On a mountain riddled with caves and crevices, the Wheel may have been purposefully situated where the sky and underground comingle—on what is called an anticlinal uplift, a spiritual interstice. Jonathan Jones writing for the *Guardian* about *Broken Obelisk* mused that where the pyramid and the obelisk meet, "Two tiny points, two zeros, touch, and immense masses are suspended on a geometrical absolute so refined it does not exist." The Big Horn Medicine Wheel could very well be predicated on just such a conceit. As a venue for vision quests, he or she who quested came to this earthwork and listened for the old spirits to volunteer guidance and insight under the stars. The spirits were forthcoming. Today these wheels, these hoops, lay upon the Earth like a Neolithic GPS of the Cosmos. The directions they give are unfollowable. The nature of address has changed, though humans still ask with their eyes and hands.

To the north, the Inuit and their cairn language, their cairnography, was ancient, too, but of transparent pragmatism. The Inuit cairn, the *inuksuk,* and its many variants have come to be a widely recognized symbol of Canadian antiquity. *Inuksuk* translates literally as "something which acts or performs the function of a person," blurring the distinction between person and Earth. Sometimes the arrangement takes a vaguely human form, the *inunnguaq*, indicating a nearby food cache or water source. Another, the *nalunaikkutaq*, meaning "deconfuser," was meant to orient the hunter or the wanderer, the seeker or the lost, amidst the snows and ice, the escarpments and scarcities. The *inunnguaq* stands like a strange troll, heralding the vanishing point. It insinuates the presence of others, the presence of intent. It is a hieroglyph. The *inunnguaq* prototypefies the spire, the steeple, the cell tower, all tall things through which voices pass.

And across the impossible Atlantic stand stones. The menhirs, the dolmens, the barrows, the mounds: more messages presaging humanity's incurable tic. They cover Gaul and the Isles, the center and the north and the south. They cover the east. A taiga of lost intent. Their fragments rest somewhat sunken in the earth. An early study for the obelisk, or a crude imitation. Follow their purpose back to the hands that teased them upward in the first place. Here is something mysterious. Something alive. Here is something that listens and speaks. These standing stones were meant, as with any technology, to *do*, to serve purpose. The nature of purpose has changed, too, though people still covet the useless, the unimplement, the untool.

Somewhere in there prehistory, that curious retronym, became history, and there were some who took notice. More markers, more monuments and monoliths proliferated across the Earth's surface. In some cases their purposes merged, or became indistinguishable. A new marker appeared, a new monument. Bright white like marble, and smooth, domed and dished and pointed, as ever, to the night. On the remote mountaintops, in the deserts: telescopes. Observatories. Recalling with little ambiguity ancient places of ceremony, it is within these new temples that present day humans channel and pay homage to the same few mysteries they always have. If science is an endeavor predicated on sacrifice and offerings—it is—then very little has changed since the Pharaohs.

The Very Large Array is situated out in the New Mexican desert, Ozymandian, its purpose upheld by a handful of poor dreaming scientists, like priests in a ziggurat, listening even deeper into the past. What do their shaman's ears hear beyond the nebulae, the supercluster, beyond the starstuff? Can they hear anything at all about themselves? Will their observations invoke, resolve, anything? Its massive dishes receive the ancient and unknown majority of the universe's noise, a soothsayer's seeming gibberish. What fanciful ruins they will make when the Earth itself is just another Smart Planet, humanity's greatest innovation, and we its Smart Life.

Pyramids, hoops, spikes, and looking glasses are all constituents of a grand technology of orientation; all appear along a continuum or gradient of mediation between an unknown or speculated universe and its human observer. Along this mediation gradient the *innunguaq* might appear far to the left, a mere footbridge between person and planet. Farther to the right, a collaboration between people and computers, might lie the VLA. Here, distance between person and planet is a bit more complicated, far less tangible, equally profound. Remember that all such artifices are sourced in the same few surface miles of one terrestrial body.

The Thirty Meter Telescope at Mauna Kea is unbuilt at the time of this writing. Historical irony charges this unfinished Hawaiian (broken) observatory because it is to be constructed on sacred ground. In a way both traditions lay the same ancestral claim, but (un)fortunately the ocean must cover at least part of the land. These, too, are prototypes, heralding ever cleverer iterations. Perhaps in the vastness the Earth itself is a marker, a relic, something we made, its emanations as obscure as they are robust, but their significance forgotten or never known; maybe Earth is the subject of hot debate amongst others out there, its ambiguities the basis of some extraterrestrial New Age. Or maybe it juts pitifully out of space's dark ground, pointed upward, weathering a lifeless quanta, a Great Silence worthy of its strangeness.

I FOLLOWED THE COAST OF QUEEN MAUD LAND for less than a day, less than a morning, with my all weather pen, my all gravities pen, circling every named outlying island and, ever the glossarist, wrote down the definitions of various obscure words for rock. Tor was familiar and so was scarp, but not yardang, not nunatak, not vesleskarvet. Those I searched in the encyclopedia. Their twists and their pinnacles rose up from the northern deserts and the southern oceans like monuments, scarecrows, familiar things. Staring at the images I also made a list of every known color. Orangutan is not a color, but I knew what I meant. I wrote amber, bad rust, hemlock flesh, Mars. Then potting soil, vacuum black, screen black, penguin black-part black. I looked at all my circled islands. Islands dot coast: that's called a loose rule, I captioned the wet, green Antarctic beaches of Queen Maud Land. In one image a nunatak stuck out from the ice like a circus tent statue. Weird rust, off-fog, I wrote. I always imagine, as I do at this moment, not exactly travelling to but materializing in such places, only to rediscover their viewless views, to rediscover the unexperience of being specifically there or that matter anywhere. At the top of the nunatak, which is a gray mesa, I am not changed in any way. I look out at a sea with many proposed names. The names are interchangeable; the waves are interchangeable. The continent is difficult, different, but well within all projections and models; the continent disappears when I hear the approach alert.

I look up from the map and see Plexaure. It is a tiny gray dot at the end of an arc. It's on a screen connected to the nav computer. It's fifty hours away. It's time to start waking up Clive, see what happens, and then put him back to hardsleep. I tuck the map and pen away in the map and pen drawer and refresh the telescopes. T2 is set to Plexaure and T1 is set to Neptune. I look at Plexaure first, and am the first, I realize, to look at Plexaure. It looks like every other little crumb-cum-moon I've ever seen; it's gray, it's battered, there are a few prominent but mundane surface features. You are going to take me around my eighth planet, I tell its gray little hillocks, its gray little cliffs, its gray little scree, its gray ancient little regolithic husk. I stick to the plan and don't look at Neptune. I look at the rubbleine face of Plexaure, across which no breeze has ever twisted, and look away. I look at Clive. Clive Cell is dreaming. The hardsleep bed monitors him and the nici presides over them, sending its stimuli. He is dreaming, and he is talking. I press Wake Up 1. I start the process. I go to softsleep for forty-nine hours and when I wake up we are in orbit and that's when I look at Neptune and see every blue and every white like an uncanny ocean covering an uncanny Earth. Perturbations perturbing, forces forcing, playing out their high but uncompelling physics. The obstinate spot in the southern hemisphere revolves and revolves and revolves as if always on the verge of becoming a whirlpool, of actual collapse, of yielding to spectacle. It never will. High altitude clouds wisp and so on, like that, but they're bigger obviously, giant actually, parasite-white and etceteran across what technically is, I guess, a sky. And that is the nature of the proposed Effect 8, Neptune Overview, for me—an elevated dread. The water I see is alien but inert, fool's tranquility, mere convulsion. I would never touch it. I look at it like I've looked at everything else, that is, past it. And past it, I think, is Muta: dark ark, apocryphal despite the data, leading its anonymous entourage of ice around the sun once every interval of shallow deep time, a blank spot, a redacted body, erasedly there. What mundane Effect 9 waits there, its supreme will to disappoint me One With the Rest of the Universe, I wonder as I watch the Wake Up progress bar creep toward one hundred percent? I let that one go. Drifting across Neptune's equator is the Chinese station from the report. *Jiaoren* it is thought to be called and it looks like a waterbug: oblong control module all dark thorax, and tubes running out of it all wandering kilometers of proboscis leading to the planet's uppermost atmosphere. It is allegedly automated. Pondlife. Unthreatening. I take the pictures and run the scans. The ship turns himself with Plexaure over and over the planet. I call him he, against obvious and legacies-long tradition, privately, to myself, when I come out of softsleep for the first time since losing count. Fifteenth time total, the computer says. The fifteenth time I woke up I gendered *Marchflower* male, arbitrarily, I think as a means of asserting eventness on the moment, as if he was my friend, something here I could call the presence of another. Once Clive is awake we'll talk. We'll look at the nici's data, discuss, synthesize, arrive at unanimous decisions, celebrate, perform rituals, we will genuflect and praise and beg and fall down on our knees, we will be spoken through and chosen and fate will lead us to the place of dawns and epiphanies and ages and paradigms and banners and feasts.

WAKE UP 1

Reindeer hooved their trails around the strip mine—up the ridges and rims, down into the valleys, between sinkholes, under the power lines, over the mosses, amongst voles and partridgeberries and pipeline, amongst the unabridged histories of extraction technology—and disappeared with the shepherds like gems and gasses from the Earth, onto its surface, across it, fed into some chamber or other, offerings finally to a dark, unmastered entropy. Spectra of changedness patterned the terrain according to viability. On one trail, high up but not so high, overlooking the giant artificial hole, Clive Cell's closed eyes nonetheless see the obvious interstice. His palms face upward; there is a machine attached to his face. His lips are parted as if mid-word. He is speaking to the wind. He is speaking to the nici.

First I dreamt, he said as he dreamt, of a fraudulent conjunction. The nici, non-intellegent, a computer, an interlocutor, limitations-associated the phrase inconclusively. I could see, Clive went on, three stars from the old days, and our obsolete hopes for them, from an impossible vantage point. Identify three stars, said—but said is such a vague word—the nici. Clive's body was very cold and slow. Minutes went by. Seconds, different kinds of silence. He said—said—finally: Kapteyn's Star, Tabby's Star, Proxima Centauri. That will sound melodious to you, that chain of names. They sound like places of importance. They're not. But there were those who wanted them to be. The old and close, the distant and different. The chosen, or at the very least the selected. The nici sends its prods and prompts and its follow-ups, gathering, gathering, vivifying.

—

Generation-predicated space travel and its narratives are beleaguered by consent: the consent of unborn children. But then, no one consents to be born in any situation, they simply are—born somewhere, on some day, to some person. I was lucky to emerge from the birth canal onto a well-worn (agate brown), possibly worn-out (expenditure brown) landmass, on a calendar day, I wrote before deleting all of it. It won't work. It hasn't in any fiction, any treatise, or any experiment. Hardsleep, softsleep, possible possibly, but they won't interface with, or solve, or even be brought to some other grand vision's all too obvious plot holes: one grand vision and its sophisms at a time. New technology, I write instead, however inchoate, however makeshift, is always put to use. This was when we passed Saturn and Jupiter without seeing them, as if they weren't there, as if we'd plotted a course through the solar system that proved it didn't exist. After Saturn a comical and fallacious quiet befell the unchanged ship and I wondered what it was when I was and was not doing everything else. The entertainment people had sent me *Pedro Páramo*, the newer adaptation, to watch, along with the usual related reading and related porn. I was watching the scene where Susana wakes up in the middle of the night and hears the pouring rain, hears the door in the next room opening, uncertain as to whether the sound means the coming or going of a person. Susana had closed her eyes again to sleep when Clive's voice came over the monitor. Look, he said, and I looked. I paused the film and looked more, waited for him to speak again, but all I heard were *Marchflower*'s various machine innuendos, the ship turned on, moving, doing. Unpause. I watched until it ended, in a hesychasmic, appetiteless stupor that overlapped the credits into a near but very much unkept-track-of future, and that was that. I realized I was awake. I was in the encyclopedia looking at pictures of cave-dwelling fish. *Amblyopsidae*, read a caption. Nervous, solitary apex predators over-adapted to near-lifeless voids. Homo amblyopsidae, I had written down. Cave-dwellers. That, I think, is the generation tech we'll have to accept: the one that leaves us absolutely behind. In this scenario, the tall ships head out to the remote planets, only to find we cannot live there as we are. So we change. We flee to the caves to escape the harsh conditions. We stay there. Our eyes adapt away, we become translucent, ever softer, our minds and intelligences themselves vestigial traits, capable only of knowing the difference between thought and not-thought. Our artifacts disintegrate, we leave behind being, we swim back into the darkness, but we make it— that way. I call it a day, an increment of conscious time elapsed, and go to softsleep for eleven days. When I wake up the first thing I think about is how wear-and-tear really occurs on a spacecraft, about cosmetic tipping points and functionality tipping points, and whether those tipping points can be reasonably predicted and graphed. Will *Marchflower* return to Mars unscathed? What has our sleep really spared it? What has it spared us, other than the bleak and atramentous inevitability of waking life? The nici has two new transcriptions of Clive's hardsleeptalk. The first one says: Here is everything other than what is. The second one, transcribed four seconds later, says: actually happening. That was nine days ago. I go to my long sleeve shirt drawer in my drawer area and release a long sleeve shirt and put it on. I feel like uninventing fire. Months pass. My interests in cave fish lead to extremophiles in general, which leads me to Antarctica. I'm always ending up in places like that. Arrivals, preparations, glossaries, Plexaure's quick phases, one Neptunerise after another, after another. We're here. Clive is waking up now.

WAKE UP 2

To say first periscope, then hatch, to say in a shallow white sea, under a fluorescent sun, that the submarine came to the surface, is to say the mind is sometimes rational, interpretable. To say he, I, Clive Cell, lifted it into the air, his, my, fingers taking hold like a benevolent, or benign perhaps, kraken, is to say something at least looked in through a porthole with a point of view. Through that tiny, watertight theater was seen a frenzied crewman staring back out—shiny face, mustache, honors-encrusted uniform, disbelieving eyes wide for the abomination outside; that crewman's flash of life, light across a night lake, epaulets, walkie talkie, his beginning, his pure endocrine terror—at me, for a split second, at my primitive heart that is visible through my chest. And then the room, its bathtub, its flood of false light works its ancient gimmick of supplanting all of it. Towels, chill, wet doorknob, vestige, residue. The esoteric passage of hardsleep has led me to this same aperture. I have not yet opened my eyes and said my new hello despite the nici's insistent pings because before I do there are a few people I'd like to thank: the god of wanderers, the god of strangers, the gods of black sheep and painted birds, the god of imposters, the gods of mutant whales and lost albatrosses, the god of paradigms, the god of discrete geological epochs, the god of the soul across its many bodies, the god of holotypes, the god of botched clones, the god of quiet telepaths, the god of anxiety, the god of nausea, the god of undiscovered islands, the god of hadal ocean depth, the god of thresholds and barriers and disputed territorial claim, the god of anomaly, the god of the contents of black holes, the god of shame and the protector of best friends, the god of glossaries, the god of the eyes of hurricanes, the god of asteroids, the god of stellar migration, the god of the expanding universe, the god of velocity, the god of the speculative boundary beyond which, nothingless and taciturn, more gods wait to be activated and adored. Gods, thank you, again, so much. Worship amongst humans is the greatest hyperobject.

CATASTROFEED

What the future
monitors my wants for is self-serving

activism

What the fuel
left to its own devices

sleeps in is darkness

intact

What the fungi
advances is delay

better loved

What the fullfillers
deprive us all of is after

after after what the comes

after the whatafter

after the afterwhat the Funnel of Love
whose swan-shaped gondola idles

and tranquilizes the harmless the
innocent Earth gravity the loyal crust

the devoted mantle harms the martyred core

After what I wait for is what I fuck for
the etceterine and the abbreviative what
waits for me always and you are
its guardian

its zinc arrow

its authenticated credential

its ventriloquism

Remember that omens are only events,
aren't real, are only movies, Jake, who is a man

I don't know well, a man who comes here once
a month, told me, And that, he continued,

if you really are an empath like you claim,
your imaginary orb of protection will make

you look one environmental pressure older
than the dawn of time

I have what I call my no-term memory set to
excerpt little bits of reality from his intermittent

advice and intermittent name and presence
Is this man's name Jake

The first echo is almost the original
and it also something new

On my face: trace evidence of every elision and
every slightly known man in my life's inner completionist

His cordial disturbances are like friends through which I might
obtain the Absolute's contact info

I ask him to interpret a very coherent dream I have sometimes
about a painter who is on the verge of becoming significant

but only to me; in reality the painter is already significant
to everyone else

Whose head isn't this stuff over, Jake asks, Who hasn't been
standing on this corner for fourteen minutes or fourteen decades

admitting to themselves that they don't know how chords work,
how words work, but that they do know a little about intervals,

specifically the interval of *I know*
Nuance in music is nucleotidal in scope

In Atlantropa the artifact farms boom
In your next few future lives you are baron after baron after baron

of things quickly obsolete, he says
I will never see you again in the present

I will see you the next time it is not March, but April
Who is Nicole Eisenman, I ask,

but he is gone again

The sharpie is mightier than our maybe
otherwise uninhabited galaxy
that like low but levitating fruit
snail mails my TV
news of dated acts of alien violence
If I connect the dots of every cool city in Canada
my fuchsia shoes will walk its eastern seaboard
all the way to the Styx's fertile delta
where I will unite against all odds
two things that make no sense together
My friend the druid records plants growing like Björk
in an anechoic chamber
It's a posture similarly, like ceremonial face paint,
like punk, like liking autumn
Sweet human sausage rises on Easter Island
to face a seawind of toddlers' breath
when you know me by the trail of sweet and sour
blood I leave behind in your bed every time
Fossil hidden water quenches my grateful death
except when I'm drafting lyrics on Tumblr
and any sound I hear that is not Enya
when Enya is playing
defaces Enya and defiles our love

GIFTS

Lukewarm tumult my iffy

fate has fastened to me:

have no curveball

antidote growing in Brazil,

no postmortem mane

or Guinness Book helix of toenails

in store for me either

Just like back off for one second okay

Rootedly astray I might be, a bit subdivided,

but the supplies of my love last

through the week   Or they can if I'm careful

These muted surroundings traject me at

what, fancifully, I call random

I repine on repeat, shampoo and shit on shuffle,

pay attention to the first fifteen seconds of anything

no matter what it is before skipping ahead

I wish I could color in the wound a bluish,

antagonized silence, make my returns to you dubiously

absolute, hinge my hands on you and find an almanac

beneath each hair

A GIBBOUS PEE MOON FOR CHIP DELANY

Before embarking in my plain white Looms
I assess what's later,
predict its warm absorptions
Its Tropical Stop Season in the tropical depression
The proto-whirl of unrest is a luscious piazza of places and waits
I make a coinish spot when I iterate
a little, when I pour salt on the brass cloud
Then, Kelp Flu comatose, my blank disk
hates the twenty minute sea between voyages,
the groundwater between graupel
They're the same though
Doppler-soaked spinnaker and the like-mint beach land puts on first
Mostly my Accordance Chip takes care of all this but
when I can, when the system is compiling and vulnerable to
malicious bypasses, and this is not often, I grind my crossed
wire down to a chalky flour
I know what makes it set
I know what makes its pH sing from the heart

HAMMERSTONE

THERE IS POETRY IN GIVING UP ONE'S VISION BY LENGTHENING IT, distending it out past death, past recognizability. When I turned thirty I left MIT and gave up on exoplanets, on Sagan, on extraterrestrial relics hanging in the dark like mobiles, Ozymandian and indifferent, their promises of sea change and revelation scattered out there in the wide, deaf galactic susurrus. I became an economist. I retired from speculation and became a speculator. A prospector. I stopped looking for big things far away. Cosmology is really just the study of scale. There's still something of that in my work. The Belt is my Cosmos, though some call it a driveway, a grind, a cul-de-sac. It's how I made my first trillion. I never thought I would hate space. But I do. When I turned sixty they needed me up there and, as always, I acquiesced. I had given ten years here and there to other things I didn't want before. Why not do it again, I mused, without a question mark so much as an ellipsis, the ellipsis in which all dreamers' schemes are fated to wordlessly pend, the ellipsis that is my totem. All the money in the world, and I have a lot of it, can't buy reliable gravity or even a nice rug, and those are really the only things I wanted for my "office." I haven't even told you what I do now, have I? I know where all the asteroids are. I pick them out, I reel them in, knap them down, suck them dry, and I work in orbit in January and February, which is very hard on my knee. Sometimes—right now is one of those times—I imagine skittering out of the Lagrange point in my preposterous monocle of an observatory and beading away into space like lymph. Adrift, starving myself as monks do, I would lower my metabolism and heart rate and self to just above zero, and very slowly, over the course of millennia, make my way to one of the Earth analogues. I'm an ambassador at heart: my true missed calling. I see the Belt as something Earthly still; roots and tubers floating through a vacuum-black consommé. What some see as mountains of platinum, nickel, and water ice, I see as radish, salsify, yuka. I'm a gatherer. Somewhere down the line my efforts will segue aloofly into the vision I've had—for myself and for the civilization I represent and participate in less and less. It's like my vision and I are moving farther and farther apart the closer I get to it, the more I age, the deeper into space's cramped cave I wriggle. That's what it feels like in here, too. It's like I've shaped the stone into plastic, woven baskets from wires, melted the mountain down to alerts and interfaces. I found a very good rock today. It's far. The op will take years. I'm leaving the giant beet to someone special in my will, in case I die. It's the biggest thing anyone has ever given to anyone else. I'm dispatching the drones tomorrow. They are the spears I hurl into each eye of the wooly rhinoceros. When it arrives in Earth orbit I will share it with my kin. I will look out across the savannah of stars and taste blood.

DEEP DOWN SATISFACTION

Add a sense of division,
add four wrists, add savagery and a flair for raw denim
Next put a decent Polaris up there
in our working Cosmos
Noble Gases, hinted-at universal
truths, and some occult for fun
like seasonal depression consequent
of Uranus retrograde
That joke has already been used in a poem
but fortunately certain jokes
are reusable and appear, like invention,
independently, often everywhere
Then add some existential mix-
up of the appendages
Add fin trapped in paw
Then add the tendency to look up longingly
at that Warmish Dot in the dark,
add the tendency to scratch that grove of serifs
roosting above the beltline
See that—beltline—things have begun to take shape and add up
Next, next add the ability to identify Maker,
add logic and roles and rupture,
Little One, add chewing my bon voyage to whatever
resultant dusky mouthful you might
I promised not to say you
Or I or to imply exactly how many of us there are
in this let's call it place
Let's just say my Work is worked and leave
it at that, at what we equal, but before our next lesson
which is about Undoing
hold up again to me your palm
that I might empty it of
embarkations

PANTHALASSA PLUS PANGAEA EQUALS WHAT

Today I will bring forth no evidence of having
done anything
Your crop of blockades and ceaseless
rustling epoxies is an odd diet
I must grow out of
because the Earth's debut shoreline
is not a somewhat level, somewhat smashed
cadmium of epiphanal detachments,
not my propolis of the periphery,
after all
What we share, what is common to us
is nothing so fanciful as air and water moving
but something much more minuscule
One obscure trauma behind a paywall of unsorted
continua
My eyes—guess where they are now—have known the
procession
of hideshirt to hairshirt like regolith to Rockefeller
My hands have known the white cliffs of Dover,
the common Earth diamond, the allspice tree, early
wheat, and the Thing that underlies them all
I'm someday specks of consensus in its calico extent
There is proof of that on my tools for transfixing
but they're from the Stone Age, earlier even,
the Stick Age
Being a born naturalist I have a motto
The sea is buxom but azygous
The one that carries
the known apart
It is no different from me

CONNECTICUT COAST IN DEEP TIME

Of all sensations
the one that stands out is panic
which, one, breathes plot
into vacation
lights of always-sprawling
August, two, dispels what antlerine
charm these lake-hugging
trees have what with my
deficient ability to witness
things period, three,
conspires the glow
out of cute sweat and cuter nightfall
and, four, keeps the scheme
of seasons breathing a labor
On this front lawn's odd
skittish universe of mellows harshed
I wipe each tremor of breeze away
like tiki torch soot from my mustache
before looking around
out at the raining random
night itself closing in
already on New London,
a horde of chill
omens from what I call the west
because it's away from the beach
inching over the estuary
I brace myself
I clench my teeth
I shovel myself whole into fear's
big T-Rex mouth
before all
those mosquito-bitten
lampoons that dam up
my haunt-starved
years spent intermittently
getting away from it all
drown me in their
sweet, sweet Off Deep
Woods, that drown me in
something on my skin
that burns, that is repellant,
that is part of the sun

THE GEOPHYSICIST'S LUCID DREAM

I was busy tapping into other realms
I was telling this one to move over,
that my promise to be the first human child
born in those primordial resorts
is the shift key I press for an alternate character
The upside down question mark, for example,
is my word you have that I am getting ready for getting out
of bed   The upside down period is more colloquial
There isn't really an oath in my English for that
It means, roughly, 'I soak the extinctions in water
overnight and push them three inches down
into Secret Garden and in the morning
when the Sun is coming up
I'm going to make them grow'
I am going to mutter them all under my breath
I am going to sign on the dotted line of eyes closed
a time lapse of every adage ever lost

UNTIL THE SUN COMES UP OVER
MCGUINNESS BOULEVARD

But I didn't read *The Orchid Thief* even though
I'd probably like it now, after the archipelago

of apartments, after all the Shelley Duvalls in *The Shining*
I've been

I did pick it up and I did keep it, carry it and never use it
like almost everything else my hands come across

behind the progress bar of the decade, there hidden
some ruinous, appropriate revelation I thought but

I was so wrong but it was fine
I had one hundred percent of my life

in my patternless head
I had done it

At Mike's house I look out the window and it's snowing
and I very much can't predict what it will feel like

to wait for my maze phase to gradually redact
my rage phase

I drink water and it never again emerges from me
I hold my palms up to what everyone has titled their visions

of earthly involvement but what is in me now can't
bring what is solid into any other state,

plain or exotic, what everything is called rests on my flesh,
a soft obstacle, strange staircase,

paranormal subplot entangling my years, my waves,
my adaptations

They do that thing where interaction of some kind leads
to a victor

I do that thing where I care kind of

I feel like the master

list of every known

suffix   Mysterious

surge of chill fission,

what is access   What is panorama

Cut the shortcut

to your impenetrable errors

Show me the long way

if it is noble,

sfumato and occult

and every interpretation that crosses my path

will be in the form of blood pressure

COMPETING AMBIENCES HAPPEN

I have

found my quaint

obscurity in the rough

inland hub

of everyone's

coordinates

CHAPTER 1

HEIGHT–BADLAND–NICHE—one smaller northern Atoll was situated on Mount Shafroth's uppermost massif, and there those that remained in the shadow of Denali, as they cast their own on Foraker, forgot Alaska. The Shafroth Atoll had five settlements, a people's council, its motions and constituents, and its citizenry. It was home to those who were outspoken and popular, and to its recluses in the lower ridges, its hermits and drifters. The Idea told the people what to do and not do, mores were passed down through the generations and between neighbors, the past was strange, and rumor was taught with uncertainty in the tiny schools. Life biased survival even at that extreme elevation, and people biased life's fabling, even if at that elevation they daily grew faint and weary.

In The Gatherer of the Hunters, a town of almost a hundred people, the Shafroth Atoll's only xylophonist and maker of xylophones lived by herself and her name was Strobilus. She shaped stone scraps of the Atoll, fiberglass scraps from the towns, ice scraps and other scraps, into the bars, troughs, and mallets of her instruments. In small, isolated communities, everyone is famous; Strobilus, though, because of her gift, was *known*.

Her studio faced the western cliffs. In the early mornings of the hot half, before the sun brought the gales, she would go to the edges of the cliffs and listen to the stormclouds' sullen, almost embittered rumbling. Louder and more articulate by the minute, the clouds approached her through the dark, over the soda flats, skittishly, as if she were a camera trap. She listened to the quickening breezes and foehns as they leapt up over the cliff face: for their dramas, for shifts in tonality. Not for voices; she knew that what came up over the rocks didn't speak like that. What came up over the rocks muttered and gasped, howled the dour errata of the lowlands, wordlessly offering to her bargains she accepted.

In the studio on a day in the middle of a mild hot half, Strobilus did not know why she was there. She hadn't needed to get anything. She sat down to eat her breakfast. The mushrooms were raw, some a deep gold color, a familiar color. The others were bluish-green, the only bluish-green in the world. A clear syrup she drank was a combination of algae and bacteria. She looked at what she had written as she chewed. The mushrooms were designed to be delicious, to taste like something she had never eaten before in her life: flesh. She didn't think about tastes, or yearn for them. No one did, because no one knew what food was. She picked up her scores for the new song and read them.

It was called *Erratic Song*, after the rubble left behind by the glaciers. The boulders, though she did insist on calling them erratics, could be seen from a distance, and reached on foot at certain times of the year; a procession of abstract and senseless monuments. She had learned the word erratic in the library; that they had been left behind by the ice, the cold. The song was almost finished. Strobilus had created a system of notation for her compositions that was part tablature, part pictograph, and there was a variation of the system for each of her xylophones, which were all unique. Schistaphone notation differed wildly from that of the gabbrophone, and each icephone had its own before becoming obsolete when, eventually, she drank them or donated them to the workshops. She ate faster. She tried to hear the movements of the song, but she could not that day; she could not focus because someone had threatened to martyr her.

On the Atoll, violence was accident. Martyrdom was abstract or arcane, ghost story or hyperbole in tremendous poor taste. The air outside was hard at work and her instruments lay around her on all sides of the room. Everything was normal and everything looked like it could be used by someone to harm her, like an obscure word, a weapon. She was afraid of her martyrer, of how different one must be to become one, or to aspire to become one. It struck Strobilus, momentarily, as revolting, a lofty type of disgust, before striking her again more plainly. She did not know that the word for this plainness of being was dread.

The mushrooms were called mushrooms, and the other sustenances had names, but they were far removed from anything that had ever grown in a forest or a field. They were automated—foolproof—failsafe. No one gave eating a thought; but they were generous with thought in respect to breathing. The mushrooms were grown in the workshops, the people grew on the mountaintop of the Atoll. Strain, a cornerstone of ecesis, was present in both populations, but the people were worse for it. In the habitat of the workshops the mushrooms had never shown change beyond the subtlest molecular level, but they were changing, wayward. She drank the last of her bacteria and left the studio quickly as precaution became panic. There was a remote battery on the north side of Hunters where she doubted anyone would think to look for her.

Power came to the towns from every direction, because it came from moving air that crossed the turbines of the Farm. The turbines were very old, but looked very new, like most of the settlements, at least from the outside, and they roared in the gales of the hot half of the year. During the warm half they turned swiftly, but made no sound. Their blades were in some motion always. The Farm was everywhere, its turbines and batteries distributed throughout the whole of the Atoll, and everyone worked on the Farm, because that was the Idea.

Teachers were still called teachers, but Farmers were called techers, and they kept the turbines and batteries going. They knew the computers. They knew how to run the crop workshops, how to rear the bacteria, and some of them knew how to use the other machines and devices that still remained and functioned. The techer called Charles Carthage had spent his minutes away from the battery on Scushen's Ridge trying to bring a very old, long disused, and widely condemned device back online: a radio. Certain that they existed, it was Carthage's desire to use the radio to contact other Atolls, but few shared his belief, and fewer his desire. Carthage's project had inspired an opposition, and its basis in fear swiftly united many people. They were afraid of being hurt, of becoming sick, of becoming hungry, and of becoming changed. They were afraid of contamination, as they had been taught to in school. Though some, like Strobilus, were unsure and remained silent about the matter, others suggested that the Idea could define his plan as a crime, and they warned him that undertaking it further might earn him candidacy for immortalization. This threat terrified him. But the radio was broken, like the world, and Charles Carthage was, after all, Steward of the Idea, and so the people came to tolerate his endeavor, trusting in its certain futility. Slowly—it took years—he became a scavenger. He studied the turbines and learned their colossal redundancies, at first repurposing their many components abstractly. Once he established that a repair to the radio was possible, he changed again. He became a thief.

Toward the end of the Height, the world's habitability had begun to wear away. The wearing away itself wore on and before long there were few places left where people could survive. Those that did hid in the mountains, high up, where it was cool, and then warm, and then hot, and then, if the mountains weren't tall enough, too hot. People rushed to build summit habitats that would last. Their isolation, once it had—over the course of decades overlapping with generations—set in, was deeply felt. It was treasured and torture, it was sacred and safety. It was Paradise. The people of the Shafroth Atoll had, in their living memory, heard of one other by name: the Samara Atoll, but all they knew was that it was far to the west, on the other side of an island chain that had since disappeared as such and which had been strung from the Alaskan summits over the sea to other summits. The islands had been the Aleutians, and the Samara Atoll was on the eastern coast, then eastern extreme, of Russia. There had been a time when travel between the Atolls was possible, routine, but that did not last long. Eventually the air became too hot, the weather too poor, eventually the means to travel deteriorated, and the Atolls were isolated from one another and reduced, gradually, globally, autotomously, to a handful of redoubts for whose inhabitants time and world were less linear and coherent by the day. Life at altitude had led to everyday problems, had made accidents worse, had complicated sleep and childbirth, indeed it had complicated all exertion. The blood of the people of the Atoll was different than it had been in earlier periods, during the Height, and the time before the Height. Their veins were different and their hearts were different. The techers who knew the hospital kept the sick well, or what was then called well, but the Atoll was often collectively dizzy and the hot imbalances of the Alaskan firmament rang in their ears for mornings and afternoons like a faint distress call. Being human, they were bound to the Earth, and though they were still on it their existence was a stretch, the bond tenuous.

Carthage lived in Bristlecone, near the library. He was a scientist; few weren't. He worked in the disciplines that life on the Atoll necessitated like everyone else: with varying degrees of aptitude. He had long ago given up the study of the heart and circulation under the stresses of high elevation, critical though it was to those whose blood would pump up there for a lifetime. He had searched the databases of the library for rumors of the world, what had been, how people had ended up on the mountain, if there were other mountains, if there were others. But he wasn't a teacher, he was a techer, and though, when he came across it, a very obscure word like wildlife intrigued him, it was ultimately other clues about the Height that he sought.

The text in many areas of the databases was badly corrupted, and the work of recovering and making sense of it was archeological by nature. There were many lucid fragments of information, tracts of nonsense, and there were intact and pristine areas that were nevertheless inscrutable. There was one reference that interested Carthage the most. It was to a place, he thought it must be a place, even before he knew it was, called Ylem Caldera. One afternoon in the hot half of the year, having finished his work on the battery that day, he thought of this place, and the woman he knew there, as he inspected his radio, which had been working for some time, a fact that he had hidden with care until about an hour before. And he thought about the woman he knew from the library, the musician.

Strobilus knew well that fewer people would be at the library if she waited until the gales came, which she always did, though she could count on Carthage to be there for the same reason. Before breakfast, she had made her way up the path and onto the porch, where she stopped for a moment to listen. When air passed over an object, when it met with resistance, sound was produced, and that sound belonged to the object like a shadow. Strobilus thought about this often as she pored over the databases in search of exotic instruments from the Height. Didgeridoos, oboes, saxophones and, more abstractly, something called a theremin were amongst the soundmakers that made up her ghost orchestra.

There was a microphone mounted next to the barometer on the porch, directly below the door kit. It was connected to a monitor in Carthage's lab, continuously streaming the sound of the air currents outside, which blew along the path to the library, sometimes keeping to it, sometimes resisting. These currents, their strength and character, varied wildly, and what came through the tiny speaker could, he thought, be their steady and coherent breath in the evening, or sudden and urgent anecdotes—tirades—outbursts—or brief, obstinate silences. He never turned it off. The air swept around the library. It was always making mention of the paths, the buildings, the mountain, sometimes with subtlety, more often with what Carthage praised as an astute grasp of the human predicament there. The air spoke of their enrangement. He had thought of that word only to discover that, at least in the library, it didn't exist.

The entrance sensed her and Strobilus had entered the library a little balefully, but froze, attentive, when through the open doorway to his lab she heard Carthage's voice answered by one she did not recognize, but knew. It was a woman's voice. Strobilus heard the voice say that the woman couldn't come to the Atoll unless she knew everyone would welcome her. Then she had heard Carthage speak. He wanted the woman from Ylem to come to Shafroth, that he could help her find the things she wanted, there on the planet, that he had written a rumor of the Atoll. He was eager to share all he knew, if she would only come. Strobilus listened. The woman was reluctant; she reminded Carthage that the orbital community did not possess the means to reach the Atoll and return home, that it would soon, but that undertaking such a trip would nevertheless be doubtful. His voice took on a desperate edge. He was trying to change her mind by changing his story. At first he reassured the woman that the people of the Atoll were ready for her arrival, then he said that a consensus would be reached soon, then that it would never be reached and that her only recourse was to come anyway. Strobilus thought she would spend the afternoon listening to him lie to her, but the woman cut the conversation off short, promising Carthage that they would speak again soon.

For a few moments the library had been silent, until the sound of Carthage bellowing in frustration coincided with an object shooting out of his lab into the library, hitting a far wall, and coming to rest intact on the floor. It was a small portable hard drive. He had emerged, his face red, breathing heavily, to retrieve it, when he saw her. She picked it up herself. She warned him that if he didn't calm himself down, he would end up in the hospital and possibly dead before he could stand trial. Strobilus had told him that he had broken the Idea by contacting the woman, and broken it further by inviting her to the Atoll. She reminded him of the consequences. The Towns would adhere to the Idea and immortalization would be on the table.

Carthage did not calm himself down. The sudden accusations aggravated him more. He grabbed the hard drive from her and she let it go easily.

She was afraid. He fumed and paced around the room, turning to her after a moment to say that he would accept, abstractly, but evade, absolutely, immortalization, that he could convince the people to welcome the woman, that the Idea didn't matter. And he begged Strobilus not to make history about it. He backed into a desk, placing one hand on a terminal, and the other, still holding the hard drive, on his chest. She hoped this meant the episode was over. She wanted to know how long his conversations had been going on, and he admitted it had been three weeks. He had first made contact only hours after bringing the radio online. She asked him what was on the hard drive. He was silent. She said she would make history about it if she had to, and he tossed the device back to her.

That she caught it was involuntary. She didn't have time to defend herself at first. He lunged. His hands were on her neck. His face was contorted, inches from hers. Though he did not speak, she saw him mouth the words *I will do it*. And there had been a moment when she thought he could. It was the moment when he thought he could, the moment when he again became something else, something worse still. She felt his thumbs crossed over her throat. He was changing. She felt what it was—stoppage—her weak spot—everyone's weak spot. He meant it. The lost postures of attack and defense, their reflexes, their routines, took on a bewildering, dejavuine immediacy. Strobilus felt the guarantee of air and the guarantee of no air. But he was too exhausted by his state. He was hyperventilating. His weakness was her ward. She pushed him, with great effort, away. He fell to the floor, and managed to say that he would make history, too, if he had to. Then he told the floor, as he rose from it, staggering toward her again as she fled the library, that the woman wasn't going to come, because for some reason she didn't want to.

The xylophone player already knew. She knew that the Ylem Caldera was a space station, not another Atoll, because she had spoken to a woman who lived there, though not that one, several times already, while Carthage was at work on the battery. And she too had entertained inviting her, had broken the Idea. But, she reminded herself, her conversations had played out differently. What troubled her then, apart from Carthage's threat, his new hostility, his sudden martyrous streak, was that he didn't seem to know, after several conversations with the woman, about Strobilus' own dialogue, just as she was ignorant of his. This of course meant the women from Ylem wanted that. Alone in North Battery, which is what the people in The Gatherer of the Hunters called her new refuge, she was glad for the first time that she had eaten, and did not know for the first time when she would again. She touched her throat. It was tender and swollen; she tried to picture the bruise, she decided it must be bad, but she was breathing normally, even after running home, and then running to the battery—reflex—response—redoubt. It was effortless. The decisions made themselves, and she made of them sense, or little sense.

The batteries were white sheds networked not to their own turbines, but to all of them, and to each other. Inside the shed, up to ten people could route and distribute power around the Atoll using a simple set of controls. This power could be sent to other batteries, individual buildings, or fed back into the turbines in the event of a possible overload. The sheds were identical, but used differently. Fresh energy generated by the turbines was managed by routing it to only a handful of centrally located batteries, which could be attended to by teams. Each town had one, and near Bristlecone another one had been designated the Master Battery, where the distribution of power throughout the entire network was monitored. The system was designed to allow for this disequilibrium. It kept the power and the observers of that power organized. It also ensured that many batteries were seldom visited.

Strobilus knew no one would be in the shed. She herself had never been in North Battery, but despite being exactly like the ones she had spent so much of her time in, the space felt unfamiliar. She approached a bank of distribution controls and looked at an overview of the battery. It was set to hold a charge between forty and sixty percent of capacity, which was standard. Energy that would exceed sixty percent was routed mostly to the central battery in The Gatherer of the Hunters, with small amounts also routed to the other towns. She noticed that additional small amounts of energy were also routed to a battery on the other side of the Atoll, near the southernmost town. This struck her as odd, though distributions of that kind often were made by mistake, or were created in the hot half for a specific purpose and thereafter overlooked. She pulled up the power scheme for The Gatherer of the Hunters, selected the building where her studio was, selected her studio, and rerouted the power to a random battery outside Bristlecone. Without power, the door to the studio could only be opened manually, with a door kit. She had taken the one from her porch. She hoped this would discourage Carthage from entering. She opened the distribution overview of the battery on the south side of the Atoll, curious about how it was being used, and thought about what to do next.

Carthage was in her studio already when the lights went out, and he knew that meant two things: that she was in one of the batteries and that she had trapped him, by design if she had taken her door kit, or by accident if she hadn't. It was there, in its housing, by the entrance. When he had arrived in the studio, he sensed at once that she was gone. Xylophones crowded the space, but there was no disarray, except on her workbench where flakes of stone and other materials were strewn wildly like arrowheads. Rage had erupted from him like a neat and steady autograph; he chose a xylophone, a gabbrophone she called it, he had seen her play it, it was the size of a small desk; he picked it up with both hands and smashed it against the wall, and the wall at that moment was his instrument, and he played on it in reprisal, or in fear, a brief song about an earthquake, a song that was over when the wreckage of keys and frame and trough settled on the floor. It was destroyed. He had then chosen another, but before he picked it up he noticed its lower keys. They were long, polished, slightly concave, corners rounded, sharp, expertly made. He had lifted one off its pin, admiring the workmanship despite himself, when the room went dark. He slipped the key into his front jacket pocket, resting it in a bottom corner. The pocket was too small. The key stuck out at an angle, pointing toward his shoulder, but he had to take it. He went to the door, feeling for the door kit. Getting it open, assembled, and turned on was easy. He was outside in minutes. The gales were weak and night was falling on the summits fast. He rushed to the library, turned the radio on, and demanded that the woman come, that he needed her, that the people of the Atoll needed her. He asked and asked and asked but she did not respond. The monitor played the sound of the air and he followed the sound, imagining a current that led up into the night, to where the composition of the world and the sky above it changed into nothing, and though he knew it could not, he imagined the current crossing that change, heading for the Ylem Caldera, for the woman, colliding with her, and bouncing back.

The woman continued to ignore Carthage; Strobilus risked no further attempts to use the radio, and no further visits to her studio. The hot half went on toward the warm half and more people were out during the day. The turbines turned. Gardens for the short season they could manage were sown and cared for. The warm half came. Strobilus would be expected to give a performance, as she always did at the beginning of the long but easier half. Hundreds of people came to The Gatherer of the Hunters to listen. She came from North Battery. In the evening, near the cliffs, she played. He was there. She spoke a little to those gathered. He watched her. The sound of the xylophones spread over the stone like shadows. When it was over, it was night. The people went home to their towns. The air moved over the mountain.

When the representatives from Ylem came, it was of their own accord, after a period of radio silence with Strobilus and Carthage, and when they did they came from the south in a tiny aircraft. It hovered over Bristlecone for several minutes, then moved off, clear of the buildings, and began to descend. The people of the Atoll stood motionless and watched the aircraft, as people who have never seen such technology would, with wonder, wonder and uncertainty, and then with fear. By the time the vehicle had touched down, the paths flurried with dust and loess as if preparing everyone present for the reveal, the first contact. But no one had remained to greet them. It was late morning. The gales came. They were strong, they weakened, they steadied. Strobilus and Carthage approached the aircraft, which was black and shiny like obsidian, from opposite sides of town, and stood before it together. They looked at each other, perhaps to each other, in shock, and did not say anything. A hatch opened, and two figures wearing masks emerged.

The figures spoke first, informing the xylophonist and the Steward that they had come, chiefly, to intervene in a situation they worried would result in violent conflict. The two introduced themselves and said where they were from, pronouncing the name several times, to clarify. The word Caldera, they added, was an artifact, perhaps autocorrected by the database somewhere along the way, most likely from Colony, but no one had ever referred to it as such, and so it could only be surmised that the entry Carthage had found in the library had been created a very long time ago, by someone who hadn't gone there. The figures invited Strobilus and Carthage to the place they had been calling Ylem, asking only that the musician come with an instrument, and the rumorian with his Rumor. Carthage did not miss that they referred to him not as Steward, but as *historian*, nor that they referred to Strobilus by name. The women must have refused his invitation because of her own involvement, her adherence to the Idea. They had no interest in him, he concluded, or the Atoll. They had come for her. His feeling of defeat lasted only a moment, but he came out of it different.

All four people knew they would go. Within the hour, the man from Bristlecone and the woman from The Gatherer of the Hunters had gone to their respective workspaces and returned. They had everything.

The women from Asylum took them into the ship, Strobilus with the schistaphone and Carthage with his Rumor on a hard drive. There was room for nothing else in the tiny cavity. Cables ran across the walls, lights and dials and switches and buckles and darkness and use covered everything like a convoluted and eons-old genome with no knowable underlying order or expression. Strobilus felt as if she were inside an extinct insect, not eaten prey, but a foreign object, a pathogen, or a disorder, as if she were something the insect was worried about or the insect's guilt. She touched her face. Her heart was not racing, but it was running. She rehearsed *The Cliff's Song*'s fourth movement in her head, eyes closed, fingertips playing her jaw, and her pulse quietened.

Charles Carthage remained motionless as the ship lifted off the ground, as it rose over the houses and the turbines, as at first one town was fully in view and then all of them, as the mountains Shafroth, Denali, and Foraker disappeared into the cloud cover. When he moved, it was slowly, a hand to his chest, where inside a pocket over his sternum he reached for the schist xylophone key, his luck, his totem, his bargaining chip. It throbbed there like an enlarged and mysterious gland. He heard her song's missing note.

The sky was a series of 'spheres and 'pauses. The road to microgravity was unforgiving of the bodies of Strobilus and Charles Carthage, such that when they reached low orbit, the two Atoll dwellers were in dire pulmonary jeopardy. High elevation—high altitude—peak height—they had known it all their lives, but now at the threshold of directionlessness their precarious adaptations were failing them. Their blood became troubled and ill, lost and in crisis. It crowded against her head and Strobilus hallucinated.

She was an origin of life. It was dark. Hot water rushed over her, but she couldn't feel it. Mileages of water pressed down on her from above, but she couldn't feel them. She was tiny, an assemblage of tininesses. She breathed easily without breath. She felt symmetrical and common, and she felt her symmetry growing, becoming structure. She felt energies entering her and she desired to keep those energies, to protect them, to use them, to deprive the world of them. She struck out at the asymmetry of the rushing water and she learned to loathe the dark while bettering herself in it. Then she left the dark. In her hallucination she knew she was much less than human, but still felt the parts of herself as if they were body parts, she knew there was a core—a vast ribbon—and barriers—between that which was her and that which was not her. She felt her nucleus. It was filled with many types of fear and they were all perfect and original. She thrived, but she desired more, she craved and starved and devoured and then ultimate and pure abundance tore through her and that was the climax and agony of mitosis—two Strobili. And then they too in due time divided, until she was surrounded by herself, a vast diaspora, a culture looking back at its zero-celled beginnings. The Strobili multiplied by the billions, and so did the years. She felt herself one being again, but she was sheless and herless, and the tralatitous significances of those billions had given way to something else. There were others there with themself, as before, perhaps like before, and they changed and reproduced, but it was different, it was after everything Strobilus knew, it was after people, and there were no words for it.

Carthage did not grasp the key, but held it lightly. The minerals and structure and resilience of that key had survived every terrestrial catastrophe there had ever been, it had been upheaved itself, removed to the farthest remotes of the world, it was inert, crustal, it was passive, it was pacifism itself, it was stone of one of the highest mountains on the planet, it had only since then borne the music of a human intellect, and now it would end that intellect, held as it was in the most savage and enduring weapon there was, the Hand. It had crossed the ranges and made its homecoming on the throat of a witness. The key underwent this transformation without the slightest segue or resistance, it would now—simply—kill—simply.

Charles Carthage was suffocating when he performed the martyrdom of the xylophonist Strobilus, who was also suffocating. He brought the schistophone key to her throat, a large key for an abnormally low note, for she had built the schistophone in the scordatura tradition, the note was designed to create a particular effect in *The Cliff's Song*, the effect of dawn in the hot half on the western cliffs of the mountain of Shafroth. He brought its fine edge to her throat and he cut, and the cells ran out of her like a bloom of red algae, like long lines of elegy, and the note that sounded told the tale of his failure better than words, because Strobilus indeed bled, and it wasn't long before they both fell into their comas, and it wasn't long after that that the women from Asylum announced that she would live.

The penalty for committing martyr was immortality. Charles Carthage knew this in waking life and in the life of his coma. In the life of his coma he awoke to exoneration, to the news that Strobilus had lost too much blood, hadn't survived, was indeed martyred, that the women from Asylum had sided with him, had been on his side all along. They told him that the Samara Atoll existed still, that it harbored a massive human population, and that they would take him there.

In the life of his coma, he convalesced at the Asylum for many weeks, healing and acclimating, breathing deeply, stretching his limbs out as far as they would go. Once he thought to look down upon the Earth in search of Alaska, but of course he could not find it. There were no shapes. There were no straits or archipelagos or basins, there were no continents. There was only the Surface. In an observation compartment, ill-fitting pieces of this revelation fell into place. Finally, after his long recovery, they were to make the descent to Samara. Carthage and two other women boarded a ship similar to the one that had met them on Shafroth. It was on this trip that he learned how—barely—such landings were possible. A larger vehicle, of which the Asylum had built but one, which they called a cusp ship, ferried the smaller shuttles into and out of the atmosphere. The cusp ship could not land. After reentry it would launch a shuttle and return to orbit. The women explained that the cusp ship had only recently been developed, and that the trip to the Shafroth Atoll was amongst its first successful uses.

The cusp ship brought them into the atmosphere and launched their lander without incident. Carthage had no sense of direction. The women told him they would approach Samara from the south. The mountains appeared in the distance, the color of his mountains, black and blue and orange and tan and white and gold and silver. He saw three great summits studded with turbines, white buildings, and long, impossible structures connecting the summits. The women told him these were monorails, a means of travelling between the settlements of this massive Atoll. They landed and were greeted by throngs of townsfolk, officials, techers, musicians, children, merchants, courtesans and lords, scribes and bards, magicians, acrobats, mimes, ewerers and pageboys, goats, ibex, and leopards, bells ringing on their exquisite bridles and sashes, bleating and snarling their welcome. They led Charles Carthage, Savior of the Idea at Shafroth, through the streets of their Farm to his reception in the courtyards of the Library of Samara, where the Cult of Chefs would invoke a dinner from the cornucopias of that prosperous Atoll. He watched as the Chefs focused the power of their minds upon the newly butchered goats—but what was a goat—roasting their haunches and legs without fire—and he watched the garlands of rosemary and saffron and dittany—and what were they—adorn the haunches—and he watched the salts of the mountain rise up from the ground and fall on the meat like snow. He watched cordials and ciders bead through the air as if in a vacuum and drip into the chalices of the harpsichordists, their robes encrusted with embroidery, their breasts sparkling with amulets. He watched the mensal knives carve the choicest loaves, and he watched as huge squashes and whelks sizzled midair in butter and parsley—as ribbons of dough crisscrossed pies that baked ovenlessly—ah, but he knew of ovenlike machines—and he watched the masters of telekinesis bring plenty to him and his brethren and he rejoiced.

It wasn't clear if the man named Charles Carthage would wake up soon, or ever, but Strobilus sat at his side in the little clinic, the long cut on her neck held fast by a foamy substance not known on the Atoll. She regained consciousness quickly, the women said, because of the way her body had mediated the two strange traumas. One woman came to her often and spoke at length while Strobilus looked out the clinic's large circular window. The angle changed continuously with the day, but always outside the Asylum was a huge, tan planet. The woman told her the rumor of the Asylum, how it worked, how they ate and generated power, and where the men were. She explained that the people who lived in the Asylum called rumor history. She told Strobilus what she knew about the other Atolls and how they were different from each other. And she returned to her the key that Carthage had taken. While the woman was gone, Strobilus slept, or thought, or watched huge patches of cloud cross the world. The schistaphone was in the room, the missing key restored to it, but she hadn't played. It was time to, she thought, pulling her chair to the window. She placed the schistophone before her, pulled two mallets from her jacket, and looked at the planet.

She played. The improvisation began slowly, not with hesitation, but as if to acquaint itself with the swaths and columns of cloud that obscured the terrain beneath. Her terrain then was in the uppermost octave of the schistophone, where she had built in identical keys that could be played to create unisons. She played these high unisons first, letting the tones ring out and fade to silence, before shifting to bright, hushed dissonances. The song, which was not a song, she knew, did not quicken or intensify, or even change much. She repeated the same few figures over and over again, until the Earth was a sliver in the window. And then she saw it.

An object had come into view, but not as the view shifted with the turning of the Asylum. An object appeared, or seemed to, from nowhere. She thought it must be an asteroid, perhaps one the Asylum had brought into orbit and mined for resources. It had the supernal look that certain geological formations sometimes did—a fantastical look that one must accept as natural with reservations, like crystal, or a natural arch, or riverstone, or basaltic prisms, phenomena she had seen images of in the library. It had the look of uncanny design. It must have drifted into her view at a moment when she turned her eyes to the schistaphone, she thought. It must have been something the women were working on. She noted absently that the object was blue. Another minute passed, and the Asylum had turned away from it, and it was gone.

She had not thought about her hallucination, about what she had been in it, and what she became in it, since it happened, but it returned to her mind now, as the door to the clinic opened and the woman came in. Strobilus shifted in her seat, turning to face her. When the woman spoke, it was with the same calm and steady tone as before. She said that she had come this time to show Strobilus something. The woman looked around Strobilus, at the schistaphone, and then her gaze shifted to the window, through which nothing was visible at that moment. Strobilus followed her gaze, and knew she must have meant the blue object, and asked the woman if that was so. The woman told her that the blue object was part of it.

They walked together to a distant part of the Asylum. Strobilus wasn't sure how much of it she had seen, but after an hour she realized it must be a huge complex. The woman talked to her as they made their way through it, passing other women along the way. She told Strobilus that the women from Asylum had made significant technological advances in the time since their habitat was first built, but that certain technologies could not be brought into use without the proper resources. She added that progress had been made in recent years, since the object Strobilus had seen in the window first started coming to Earth. She explained quickly that it was not an asteroid, that it was not natural, nor was it unnatural. Strobilus didn't understand. They arrived in a deserted observation deck, its window into space much bigger than the one in the clinic. Through it, huge, very near, was the blue object.

Before Strobilus could ask, the woman told her that she did not know what it was, and that furthermore, the unknowness of the object outdated such questions. It did not represent a technology. It was not a vehicle. It could be a vessel, as a cup is a vessel for water. Nor, she went on, was it crewed, though, the women—bearing in mind the absence of a better, more appropriate vocabulary—conversationally used the word *someone* to describe what was there. The woman confirmed that the object appeared out of thin air, as Strobilus had seen earlier, remained near the Asylum, and vanished again, every sixty five to eighty hours.

She told Strobilus that the object—she paused often, using certain words as if against her will—*went* back and forth between Earth and another—another pause—*planet*, but that went and planet were not exactly accurate. She admitted that the women didn't know how it worked, but that they had gone with it to this other location, and that they wanted to take Strobilus there. The woman explained that they had some—pause—metaphors for what could be—taking place. One important and difficult consideration was that the vessel did not, as she mentioned before, seem to make use of what people called technology, but rather a technology-analogue. It appeared to have functions that were like the functions of their own spacecraft, insofar as it had a form, was partly—pause—a habitat, and was designed to—and here she paused again. The temptation was always to say *move*, and she said they often did say that. But the vessel didn't propulse. It—managed—distance—and apparently only one single distance—by some other means. Words like traverse or cross or cover were words they avoided. The object remained outside the window. They looked at it. After a short silence the woman said that they called it their Albatross. And that some called it their Person. It would remain outside the Asylum briefly, and then—depart. The woman would go with it, and so could Strobilus, if she wanted to.

She did. The woman told her the preparations had been made and that they would go to the object. Boarding the tiny shuttle, Strobilus was again reminded of her hallucination, and Carthage's attack, but with detachment. She realized she did not know how long it had been since she had come to the Asylum. She touched the plastic scar on her neck. It didn't hurt. The shuttle left the Asylum and moved toward the blue object. For a second she saw the Asylum. It was enormous. And as they pulled away from it, and the field of view became wider, she saw other complexes. She saw a giant asteroid in a silvery vice. Tiny lights shone in its mineshafts. In a few minutes, their shuttle, the *Lacuna*, had nosed up to the object, into a sort of hollow or niche in its side, if it had sides. There was a jolt as the *Lacuna* attached itself to the object. Strobilus asked the woman when they would leave, and she said only that leaving wasn't accurate. They waited.

Waited was accurate. After many hours in the shuttle, without warning or preamble, they were somewhere else, a fact made obvious by the planet that appeared in the window—a planet not Earth. It was huge and close. Strobilus felt nothing of the uncanny, no sensation whatsoever, only that one moment had passed to the next. She breathed normally. She kept silent, waiting for the woman, who said nothing at first. They were alone over strange clouds. The woman spoke. They couldn't land there; it wasn't that kind of planet. Possibly, it wasn't a planet at all. Beneath the swirling gasses that could be seen from orbit, there were structures, possibly geological, possibly artificial, but the data were ambiguous in either scenario. It did meet certain criteria in terms of how planetary bodies were defined—it was a round celestial object that seemed to have been created as a byproduct of stellar formation, for one. But other facts didn't add up as neatly. It wasn't where it should have been in the system, and the system itself seemed to be returning to equilibrium after a period of sudden, inexplicable change. It was the woman's opinion that the planet, or whatever it was, had been moved somehow, that the balance of the system had been adjusted, or manipulated.

Strobilus listened. Other blue objects appeared in orbit with them. At first only a few, then many more, then more than she could count. The woman talked through the spectacle. The women thought of the phenomenon in terms of what they called a migration architecture. The objects seemed to arrive there, or return there, periodically, as albatrosses or penguins used to convene on islands in the southern hemisphere on Earth. Sometimes the women arrived first, sometimes there were thousands of objects already there, other times millions. Sometimes their Albatross left early or late. They had observed some go into the planet. They didn't know where the others went when they vanished. They did know that when they were near the other planet, they were far from Earth. Their instruments could find no recognizable points of reference in the stars by which a proximity to Earth could be ascertained.

Objects crowded the view. And then the view began to shift. They were moving toward the planet. The atmosphere glowed. They passed into it in silence and the *Lacuna* was filled with light. Strobilus looked at the woman, who smiled at her and said that human beings learned to recognize abundance early on. The primate brain was attracted to and obsessed with presentations of abundance. Strobilus nodded. They emerged from the cloud cover and there were so many objects surrounding the planet that space was no longer visible. They could see only the blue of the Albatrosses.

CHAPTER 2

The wind with its perpetual

rhetoric was searching

for answers in the canyons

and the trenches, in the endless bunkers of desert

ants, in the taigaland's brittled stickdom,

at the feet of mountain ranges

It swept up the loamy but inert earthstuff,

showed it

in the sky, and randomized

it down again

And the mountains rose up

out of this

randomization like reefs

The valleys were the valleys

of death, and the shelves were the shelves

of death, and the same was true for the channels

and the floodplains and the buttes

The gasses and their speeds were

the wind and the answers answered:

Exonym—echo—edge—elegy

Because that is what search sounds like on bare stone

ONE BASIC UNIT OF LANDMASS ON THE CONTINENTAL SCALE is the craton. A craton is an abnormally buoyant segment of the Earth's crust that, owing to it's low density and particular composition, bobs on the mantle and forms landmasses by a process of accretion. This process began, it is thought, during our planet's Archezoic period, roughly four billion years ago. It continues today and is driven by something called, by turns, plate tectonics or continental drift.

The lost continent is an obsolete trope of human dreaming. Though much of the Earth remains remote to people, that is, to individuals and civilizations, there is a big—low resolution—picture of the sprawling speck we inhabit. The human species has never lost a continent once in its evolutionary history, but it has found and fabricated many. Over the desolation of eons that obscurely prefaces consciousness, the jigsaw of primordial cratons walked the water of the Earth in their phlegmatic, unknowing way. The great and small islands and seas scattered and coalesced, did and undid themselves and so set the varied and mysterious stage known today as the world.

Pangaea, Panthalassa, Tethys, Gondwana: these and others make up the geologic pantheon of lands and seas in deep time. What sounds very much like a mythology actually is not; though the real in this history has been named like a cast of capricious titans, the clash and scatter in this case really happened, imperceptibly, so long-taking in fact that it looked like it didn't. But the names and 3-D models are there, waiting in the crevices like predators. Who are these oceans, these super and micro continents on which historians and scientists have imposed their mythbuilding? The very act of animating them with these names seems unscientific, unobjective.

Consider what else populated those crevices. Anything so ancient is ostensibly the stuff of cryptozoology, that fashionable flight of nostalgia: giant sea moth, abominable swamp man, Loch Ness T-Rex, Jersey jungle walrus. Even what we know to have been real is as good as imagined, petrified in the fossil record of fantasy. Flightless dragons walked the Earth back then that would evolve into a kind of gilled mouse. Aquatic wolves with eyes looking up from the top of their skulls would evolve into whales. The Earth always manages to prove its far reaches if, as with people, given time.

The lost continent myth originated in minds perceiving a world not yet mapped in full. Even then, as close as we were to having everything, we yearned for more. It was at this turning point exactly in our imaginations that we out-paced the physical world, the plates and basins and faults and trenches, when a certain part of basic, achievable discovery became unsustainable. The stock of the undiscovered retreated, like whales, to the poles. The thrills became as featureless as those places and the world was ours.

Two billion years ago several cratons were clustered together, forming a con-tinent formally named, in 1996, Atlantica. These cratons then separated and part of Atlantica became what would eventually be South America; another, what would eventually be West Africa. As the landmass fragmented an ocean began to pool in the spaces between them—the Atlantic Ocean, named for Atlas, a second-generation titan in Greek mythology.

No craton, however fancifully named, carried away Atlantis. But it does exist, spectral and tantalizing, in the hearts of many like a phantom limb floating in a brand new Atlantic. That ocean is deep, full of mysteries and fictions, names and designations, Greek roots and wrecked ships, the mindless alive and the dead forgotten.

In 1836 Hans Christian Anderson wrote "The Little Mermaid," shortly after Charles Darwin arrived in Australia and saw his first platypus. The mermaid genome would tell a similar story as that of the platypus—one of barrier-cross-ing, plurality, rupture. Indeed Anderson and Darwin, looking upon an imag-ined species and, respectively, a real one, saw the same thing, felt the same fascination. One hundred and fifty-three years later Walt Disney released its animated splashterpiece *The Little Mermaid*, based on Anderson's story. The heroine of the story, Ariel, is a mermaid possessed of the human urge to trans-gress. She is tired of being a myth and a sighting, bored with her royal role in the underwater kingdom of, you guessed it, Atlantica. Denizen and diva of the deep, citizen of the void left behind by unfeeling cratons, she wants more. She wants to be part of your world. To want something is the first step toward becoming human and it might be the only step.

The song "Part of Your World" was co-written by Alan Menken and Howard Ashman for *The Little Mermaid* and it barely made the cut, which is difficult to imagine now. In the opening of the song Ariel looks over her coveted, name-less human relics. Though useless to her in their alienness, those sunken forks and candlesticks are part of her. They are the source and core of her desire, the wreckage that drives her to air, birds, the cratons, and eventually, at no small cost, transformation. Throughout the song Ariel struggles with a vocabulary consigned to land-dwellers. She must conjure the words feet and street from their distant, dry, ambulatory realm. The word burn for her is purely meta-phorical and theoretical, but she feels these meanings within her as if with real temperature and combustion, as if the embodiment and change she wants can be learned like a language, as if she were unbound by what she consisted of physically.

Time consists of increments, the voice consists of registers, and song consists of all four of those things, but can only be brought to life by the third. Laying claim to a song by singing it is a harrowing endeavor. At Howard Ashman's memorial service, Jodi Benson, the original singer of "Part of Your World," recalls promising the deceased to get the phrasing just right. During rehears-als, Ashman urged Benson to sing from an "inner intensity"—Ariel, after all, sings the song in a secret underwater cave; a kind of sanctuary embedded even deeper in a general Atlantican claustrophobia. This intensity is also, presum-ably, the one that comes, as a writer, from ownership of a song, and from, as a singer, a successful stewardship of a song. How difficult it must be to embody a song, to fit oneself to it, and yet the traditional and the popular song, the covered song, are as old as song itself.

"Part of Your World" has been widely covered and re-recorded. For his sub-mission to Broadway World's 2007 "Give Us Your Voice" competition, vocalist Nick Pitera, whose YouTube videos would subsequently go viral, sang a ren-dition of it in his signature, near-ineffable falsetto. As the song begins, it is instantly apparent that Pitera has closely studied the video in which Howard Ashman coaches Jodi Benson during rehearsals for The Little Mermaid. He knows that the falsetto register, with its whispery textures that can clear up and expand to a siren-like wail, lends/gives itself to the song.

In the opening lines Pitera sounds of ambiguous sex, an ambiguity that per-sists through the performance and is central to its power. The restrained, al-most whispered lines shift to a wail and return again seamlessly. It is only in those moments in the first half of the song when Ariel searches for words that Pitera reverts to his speaking voice. "What's that word again?" he asks, ordinarily, before singing the answer in utter contrast, as if the answer is in his voice, his treatment, his physiology. Here, falsetto becomes fiction, his voice a vehicle for transformation. Alternating registers, Pitera toys with the notion that the realms he inhabits are really so far apart. Man and mermaid, he wants to win. As the song builds in (inner) intensity, Pitera's voice utilizes the whisper less and less, right through to the song's central question, "when's it my turn?" At this point Pitera is singing away from the camera, through the foam walls of the vocal booth, through kilometers of water, though the ocean's roiling surface, straight at what lies beyond reach, and in the last moments of this crescendo, in fact at the precise moment he sings the word "love," he looks exactly like Tilda Swinton in Orlando. Her/himself an English ambas-sador abroad in the Middle East, Orlando, immortal, changes sex in Virginia

Woolf's astounding work of science fiction. "Same person. No difference at all," Orlando says, because the stuff of myth and self know no boundaries.

—

In 1945 on a volcano on an island called Iwo Jima, far from any craton but slightly above sea level, a man named Joe Rosenthal took an iconic photograph. Fifty-seven years later Mariah Carey sang the Star Spangled Banner at Super Bowl XXXVI and she, too, shares in the legacy of that ill-fated volcano, in the mystique of its overtaking. Though it may be true that the United States relinquished its occupation of Iwo Jima in 1968, it will lie dormant under that black and white flag so long as the photograph persists in national memory. The YouTube video of Mariah Carey singing the Star Spangled Banner at the Super Bowl is a historical document. Like *Raising the Flag at Iwo Jima*, Carey is an American icon, possessed of her own mysteries, power, allure, illusion. It was thought (by some) that Joe Rosenthal's photograph was staged; it is accepted that it was not. It was thought (by some) that Mariah Carey's performance was pre-recorded; it was.

Like "Part of Your World," "The Star Spangled Banner" was written by a songwriting team. The lyrics were sourced from the poem "Defense of Fort M'Henry" by Francis Scott Key and, omitting the last three stanzas, fit to a pre-existing composition by John Stafford Smith of London. The resultant anthem, cobbled together as it was, reunites the Empire and its Colonies in an utterly inevitable, discombobulated coherence. As the song begins, the land at stake is up for grabs, unclaimed, unconquered, awaiting sovereignty. The Americans sing their poetry to a British tune and prevail. Key's words captured that candid victory and sent them into the future like a probe collecting all the good data of patriotism.

Mariah Carey is famous for her ability to sing in the whistle register, known in vocal pedagogy as the flageolet, the highest register reachable by humans. Like Nick Pitera's uncanny falsetto, the quality of Carey's whistle is a gift—melody is a signature they sign in voice. Though her particular vocal vocabulary can be heard throughout her rendition of "The Star Spangled Banner," the high note is always the obvious standout: B6, which is also in the vocal range of dolphins. The note is so high that the word "free" is free of enunciation, unpronounceable, in the minds of the listener only. In true American form, Carey lays claim to the song's territory, crowning herself queen with every echo of "Dreamlover" she embeds in the melody, every square inch of the fantasy and loss that makes up so much of her own work. Like "Always Be My Baby," "The Star Spangled Banner" celebrates earned reclamation. When Carey's voice soars into the whistle register like a rocket, like a bomb, she knows that all matters of time have finally made their homecoming.

It remains uncertain if Carey can get there on command. Her Star Spangled Banner was pre-recorded. Other notes in the whistle register are sometimes overdubbed into her live performances. It's like a fickle muse. In the moments leading up to the legendary B6, the camera abandons Carey and instead circles a sculptural replica of Joe Rosenthal's war photograph, uncannily, just when evidence for that impossible note is most urgently desired and available. Because the note is inaccessible, unbound, Unreal. It has been told of and sung but not observed. It is a myth. According to some exotic cycle outside the purview of humankind, its filaments rise slowly from the volcano on a curl of rock mixed with minerals mixed with glass. Ash.

—

Someday science will describe Dark Matter and give it a new name. Probably the word "Dark" will be replaced by some clever person's last name: Yarrier, Frossing, Nork, Dender, Pictory, something like that. For now, the study of Dark Matter is cutting edge physics, distinct from fringe physics and pseudophysics, which are branches of pseudoscience. The field of pseudoscience is bright with invention and forefathers, just as the field of science is bright with dreamers astute and dreamers foolhardy. The spectra that unite these traditions are as empirically, fabulously convoluted as the brains that conceived them. There are scientific truths, foundations that, like cratons, form the basis of how the human species understands the natural world and the universe. There are also pseudoscientific truths, pseudofoundations, pseudocratons around which accrete falseness and delusion. The British Isles are closest to the geological craton formation known as the Baltic Shield. Every landmass on Earth is situated on a global pseudocraton called Apate, named for the Greek goddess of deceit. Maine, of course, is on the fringe of the North American craton, and it was there that Wilhelm Reich imagined Orgone Energy and its counterpart, Deadly Orgone Energy, a cosmic force entangled with human sexuality and rain, a kind of Dark Matter chauvinistically linked to libido.

Wilhelm Reich moved to Maine in 1942, after being mistaken by the FBI for a communist bookseller in New Jersey. Though suspicious, his notions about Orgone Energy posed no threat to the United States of America. He was largely thought to be a fraud, had ties with Albert Einstein, and a very questionable collection of books. He named his farm Orgonon after his energy. Suddenly, that ordinary plot of land carried new weight. On this farm, Reich experimented with controversial devices he called "cloudbusters," which he claimed could focus Orgone Energy in the atmosphere, inducing rainfall.

Peter was there when the FBI arrested Reich. Peter, his son. This traumatic event is the subject of Kate Bush's song, "Cloudbusting," from *Hounds Of Love*. Bush portrays Peter in the music video. The song, written from Peter's point of view, recalls the day Reich was taken away, his laboratory ransacked, his work confiscated. "Every time it rains / you're here in my head / Like the sun coming out / I just know that something good is gonna happen," Peter/Bush sing. The sense of the chorus is one of a pathetic fallacy in reverse, inverted nostalgia, futility blown so out of proportion that it resembles promise. In writing this song, Kate Bush looks across the Atlantic Ocean, into the past, into the life of a child, into the future of that child—and at that advanced stage of speculation decides to take hold, to embody. Who is Kate Bush but the son of a mad scientist? In the world of the music video, but after the action of it, Kate Bush as Peter wanders the fields of Orgonon, abristle with decaying cloudbusters. They point upward like deaf weeds, finding nothing, performing no task, facing the cosmos uselessly like the stone heads of Easter Island. They have no significance. In Old English there is a single word for the feelings inspired by looking at ruins. The word is *dustsceawung*—dust-seeing. Kate Bush as Peter looks at the cloudbusters. Shel Silverstein, rise from the dead and draw me a picture book about that.

During a performance at New York City's Webster Hall, the song "Cloudbusting" was covered by singer/songwriter Solange Piaget Knowles. Knowles as Bush as Peter cannot protect Reich from the FBI. Knowles as Bush as Peter hides the yo-yo in the garden. Knowles as Bush as Peter chases the car down the country road until it vanishes into the hills. Knowles as Bush as Peter runs up the hill and activates the cloudbuster and it works because it is real and the sun is shining and the truth is finally revealed. Knowles fits herself to the song and approaches the coda like a coyote and climbs the step-pyramid to the final note. The note is high, not dolphin high, but high enough. She has shifted shapes. From the top of a step-pyramid lost continents become more abstract. A house is a lost continent. A street, a shape, a chord change is a lost continent. Darkness is a lost continent. A time of day, a bad idea, an area code, two particular colors next to each other, a catchphrase, a knickknack, all these are lost continents. Everything impossible to forget is a lost continent. Fathers, sons are lost continents. That which is obsolete and that which is useful are lost continents. The future is a lost continent. Names are lost continents. Fondness is a lost continent. Kate Bush's first piano is a lost continent. America is a lost continent. Verifiable truth, death, meaning, God, the origin of life on Earth, the universe before the sun, whatever came before the universe and whatever will come after.

—

The word nostalgia was coined by a Swiss medical student approximately one century after the invention of yodeling. It described a condition suffered by mercenaries living abroad, whereby the patient, upon hearing simple, traditional Swiss horn melodies called *Ranz de Vache*, would experience desertion-inducing homesickness. Whistling these melodies was prohibited under Swiss law. From the Greek words for homecoming and pain, the notion of nostalgia arose from music and pathology.

For his blind audition for the *The Voice of Italy* in 2014, contestant Tommaso Pini sang "Summertime Sadness" by Lana Del Rey. Like "Part of Your World," "The Star-Spangled Banner," and "Cloudbusting," "Summertime Sadness" is a nostalgic, commemorative song about having something and not having something at the same time, a conceit dear to the human psyche and suited to music's home dimension of time. The immanent separation chronicled in "Summertime Sadness" is colored by equal parts melancholy and thrill, Del

Rey's hallmark emotional confabulation. When Pini begins to sing, it is as when Nick Petera begins to sing. Who is it? The judges in their garish thrones sit with their backs to him. Is it a him? The beguiling androgynous croon befuddles the viewer, too, because of the way the show is edited. It's a double mystery, a quadruple mystery, an infinite mystery. The judges nod knowingly, exchange meaningful glances, spin around and behold Pini at the height of his performance of this devastating *Ranz de Vache*, of the anthem of pain Del Rey fabricated for herself, that the feedback loop of loss's joy might never abate. In "Summertime Sadness" the separation is always about to happen but never does. That stalemate is the dark craton of desire, of war, of the past. No matter how hard we try, these barriers are insoluble in thought. What we want and what we need staggers though the breadth of the human register. There, nothing else matters, let alone exists, let alone is open to debate. Maybe it's reality TV or maybe it's something someone calls their art. Maybe it's all just cosmic rays planlessly workshopping our genes into gibberish. But what is certain, what the evidence shows, what is undeniably in the data, what is conclusive scientific fact, is that the greatest, most lost land of all is ourselves.

CONTACT

I open the folder called Fake Places

I open the folder called Early Impressions

I open the folder called Last Ditch and skim through the Infinite

Jest of my life and find nothing,
some nothing with which I might at least work
Who has time to solve my tall Troy walls
Who believes the fandom's protective mystery will save my fads from undead metaphor
If the undead metaphors pour in and over them
I have time to involve the act of *parsing*, to put my lips to the coronet and sound the error,
throw the error, whatever it is, accordingly
If the trolls and incomplete strangers cake the bazaars with their empire-declining antics,
then victory, defeat, they'll be rumored and debunked, authenticated in the provinces no
matter what happens or happens
The coronet is somewhat trumpet see
A slim cairn see
A comet tail of days avoided toppling see
out of my mom
Overthrown, over sound, beyond error,
my escape is a matter of control
X and V but never C
The same goes for my return

I open the folder called Things I Love And Know every day
And there is my super commonness
in a common universe
And there is my super commonness' finger poised
over the folder called Black Hole
It hovers precariously
It will press matter
at its center and wait
for something that is never me
I open the folder called Growing
As Green And Voluptuous As This New World Did
In All The Ages Up Until This One Within It and within
it the common universe shies away from everything I've learned
about science fiction

I open the folders called Primitive Needs and Primitive Satisfactions and they are empty
I open the folder called Knock Knees and find the whetstone henge that remains of my
druid-built, druid-abandoned sex drive
Like other such sites I am unsearchable and have no name
No name, but messages, strange messages
No druid, because what is a druid, but remains, strange remains

Critics call space griddy and axes-packed
Seed vaults weird me out
Ozone clouds the crystal ball with mystery
Gaze into my Earth
I'm presoaking the future
(You're invited to its séance)
In a sacred river's profane delta
My spirit horn's modest range will break up the stains
And together we will summon up and collate every stock genetic koan

Sometimes I wonder what a life spent studying ants
and believing in God must have been like
I spent my life interpreting its decades and living with various
ADDs, untreated
Sheryl Crow spent the sentiment in the first line of Run Baby Run, where she's like
I was born the day Aldous Huxley died, on never returning to it
No one cool died
the day I was born
My life, Sheryl Crow's life: where are they at
My point is the only thing Adderall is the key to
Adderall is the key to my point and nothing else
O sprawling, aureate Smashing Pumpkins song five hundred times in a row,
fail to open the Doors of anything amen
O chemtrail across the Absolute
O urethra across time ew sorry
Go ahead
Kick me out of the band
I'll find the blood that freezes at ninety seven degrees or four hundred fifty
I'll build my space station in low orbit over Mercury
I'll be like the guy in Sunshine directed by Danny Boyle
A shouting beef-jerky golem subsisting on hydroponic lettuce
I will have such visions
Infinity, bursting with flavor, will come to roost
in my voice

★★

The expanses suffer slow old-fashioned battery death

Not gory exhilarating bursts

No transmission-ending dark theory bloodying the lens

But AbEx and Endgame, perhaps
A touch of purpose
It will look like that
A big patterned field
One trillions-fold empty entry
But until then here is my shrine to the Great Galaxies
My kinetic aplomb of resigned wonder
Redundancy and rove
The side-species that is guesses
It can't be denied that a guess is something truly alive
That's the weird thing about science
If inertia is a form of propulsion
Turns out I have no meaningful ownership of any symbol

I told myself that when I got this far in life everything would break
down, slow down, become nebulous and neurotic like Maurice
Blanchot novels
You'd better believe that was just another promise kept in the X folder with
the first acoustic guitar in space burning up during reentry, its sooty trail
of basic chords reshuffling, renothinging
O carbon patina you disappear into the home planet's ultramarine urn of
secrets and lies
I open the folder called Secrets + Lies
and inside is another folder called Human Invention and inside that is yet another folder
called False Devotions and inside it, finally,
I cultivate them

I mean there are other Tropics than the dumb Zodiac
ones Henry Miller named those books after
The Tropic of Fascia of Camper, which cuts across New York
The Tropic of Perineum, which cuts across southern California
O tantalizing anatomies
O tantalizing slime mold map
O Object Oriented Ontology I am your biggest sycophant
I name lines after other things, too, and in the name of other things
I wrinkle time
I cast a shadow over all human discourse
O southern New York
Do you exist
O southern Xanadu
Are you an RPG I spill blood in when I robotrip
The world rotates on its axis like a slow, torturous gif

I open the folder called Watermelon Sugar
and inside it the unfinished screenplay smiles up at me unfinishedly
I estimate the decay rate of utopia in open ocean, then in dirt, then in
controlled compost
I imagine a Great Pacific Utopia Spiral
Particulate utopia caught in the gills of fish and the lungs of birds,
breaking down into smaller and smaller pieces of the same
one thing
I imagine utopia collapsing the whole world
one species at a time until only humans remain
I imagine fighting it to the death and winning

SETI is the great tragic love story of sentience

I open the folder called Summers
and in one of those whenever whatever ones
maybe three or four or eight or nine ago
Borna and I are on the highway in Corona
during the tornado
The air is green and whipping and everything you hear people
say about that stuff
At any rate we are en route to Oxford, Connecticut
to a defunct satellite television facility a friend recently
repossessed to pick up many small TVs
It is hot
Really hot and I feel like I am diminishing
We go up onto the roof to climb on the giant satellite dishes
I feel like Alfred Noyes though I bear no torch
I feel like Laura Linney in Congo though I bear no
diamond-powered laser
I point up at the sky and fire anyway
though I have no vendetta to visit upon anyone
or anything except
my own all-consuming powerlessness
Borna is wearing the Converge t-shirt this month
I can hear Converge thrashing though the one hundred percent
daylight, the one hundred percent comparative stillness
I hear dissonances ordering this weird opposite
of New York, dividing the wind and heat
and odyssey and ludicrousness of the whole day
into a different set of repeating seasons
I feel a riff reason straight through me to the other
side and resolve
The UV Index was high
I longed for miserable winters
For objects so cold and distant I would never
even know they existed

I open the folder called Aimfully
I open the folder called Potential Agendas
Needle sparrow, smog sparrow, smog swallow, distortion sparrow
I listen to the loud sound of hidden people
and I swear I spend no time wandering around their fates

★★★

There is a type of grief that can be upcycled

Into just feeling kind of shitty-chic

On its anti-epic slalom we are

Heirs to the isthmus that repairs
Fixation
The next to never rate of Reason
Back when every hayseed savant
Could rebuff say gravity
Back when there weren't no phones
Back when you'd never hear from a person again
I was in my prime then

Whatever is the om I concuss
into every starry night's
wide overture, every science
poorly understood, every ire itemized in that big wonderful
invoice in the sky
Whatever is my alternative to Celsius and Fahrenheit,
Batman and Robin, Leopold and Loeb, Ren and Stimpy,
drum'n'bass, Kavalier and Clay,
Law & Order, Siskel and Ebert,
space and time, love and death
Inside the folder called Whatever, well, is a few paragraphs
from Carl Sagan's Pale Blue Dot, which contains everything,
which describes that which houses and shelters everything,
our unique, particular and highly finite everything
What is inside everything
Such magnificent remains
What magnificent remains
What remains

I open the folder called Infinite Jest and close
it immediately
I have done this many times
O I know nothing
O we're best friends

I feel like Jodie Foster as Eleanor Arroway closing my cricket cage door
My slingshot to Vega buffering in an astronomer's novel written in the 1980's
I am loading Earth with a spring
The Overview Effect truly is a kind of Nirvana
song compared to the pandemic butthurt that is life on the continents
You should come to my whole planet house party
You should bring beer
You should bring Ryan
I keep saying you but the big black chance of space will not answer
Probably

I open the folder called My Voyager: My Lonely Total
and it's kinda weird
Please have some form
of worthwhile, oncoming
mystery, oh missing techno
of my farthest
reaches
The long ambiguous tundra between us and everything else
is the only thing between us and the long ambiguous tundra
of everything else
Along the way I have taken lots of pictures and listened
to a lot of noise music too
and after my under-estimated span of whatever this is
I, too, will shut down for good but I will still do
what I always have
I will drift unrecoverably

Odysseys to be had that are not procedural: are they there?

I'm not sure who I'm asking what and vice versa, or what who

Bad Inventions: satellites, graphic representation, seasonal change, migratory patterning,

planetary accretion, the chemical elements

Hello, I'm here

My Sunlight Locater shows me everywhere it is day

The Book of Communist Pleasantries excludes *How are you*

and so does the Book of Ambiguous Democratic Pleasantries

After the news breaks, I offload all the continents' comments,

offland them, that is

Every abnormal location invokes what I'm trying to avoid

which is why my algorithm generates familiar locations only

But the clear coast is a part per million amongst, what, risky, hazardous coasts?

I see them coming over the horizon like Harmattans of anthrax and cocaine

Here's my house key now

I'm ready to hold it up and relive my golden, lost minutes

This is going to be a turning point for the concept of bereavement

I can't wait to think less about fate and destiny

when I imagine that the spade—which I don't think I have ever seen in real life—

in my hand—and I can barely imagine my own hand—

penetrates what I have read

is called dirt, creating with prowess, with purpose,

a perfectly useless

lacuna

in the Earth

NOTES

The title of "Loud Spring" refers to Rachel Carson's book *Silent Spring*.

"An Earthlike Planet For Ianthe Brautigan" owes something to a passage about Kurt Cobain in her memoir *You Can't Catch Death*.

"Impact Crater" is for Julien Raffinot.

The opening sentence of "Plexaure" echoes an anecdote related in Douglass Botting's *Island of the Dragon's Blood*.

The poems "A Dedication Theory For Sekou Sundiata" and "New York Eternity" reference the songs "On The Beach" and "Pocahontas," respectively, by Neil Young.

The insights in "Last Lost Continents" concerning *dustsceawung* and nostalgia were sourced from Melanie Challenger's incredible book *On Extinction*.

ACKNOWLEDGEMENTS

I would like to thank the editors of the following magazines, in which many of these poems and stories first appeared: *Luna Luna Magazine, Berfrois, H_NG-M_N, Diner Journal, Poem Tiger, BORT Quarterly, SciArt Magazine, glitterMOB, Forklift,Ohio, Queen Mob's Teahouse, Terraform, Dark Mountain, Big Echo: Critical Science Fiction, InDigest, nin journal, HARIBO, Sundog Lit,* and *Tagvverk.*

A few other pieces originally appeared in a chapbook called *Executive Producer Chris Carter*, which was published by The Operating System in 2014.

"Six Large Holes" was selected by Jeff VanderMeer as a runner-up in *SciArt Magazine*'s first flash fiction contest.

"Tropical Premises" won first prize in *Terraform*'s Post-Human contest.

"The Women From Asylum" began as a response to Arthur C. Clarke's "Exile of the Eons," and was written for a special issue of *Big Echo: Critical SF* about the legacy of his short fiction.

GRATITUDE

Help is other people. There have been many who have shaped this book,
none more profoundly than Anna Dunn. I would also like to thank
Phil Anderson, Andrew Daul, Claire L. Evans,
Steve Wheeler and William Squirrel
for their insights about the stories.

Of course there is more to it than that.

Robin, it was your idea.
Lynne, there are no, and only, words.
My parents: a Cosmos of gratitude:
all that is, and ever was, and ever will be.
And in my daily life, which is the same as my whole life,
which has nothing to do with any of this, but also is all of it,
thank you, Benjamin. I love you so much.

And to UKL:
I will make whatever I am in break free of time
and take me out across the darkness.

POETICS AND PRACTICE
PMG IN CONVERSATION WITH LYNNE DESILVA-JOHNSON

Greetings comrade!
Thank you for talking to us about your process today!

Can you introduce yourself, in a way that you would choose?

I'm PMG and I'm a travel writer. I'm from Massachusetts, where I was born in the valley and raised in the hills. I live in Brooklyn and I work at a hotel.

Why are you a poet/writer/artist?

Part of me wishes I knew; part of me hopes I never find out.

When did you decide you were a poet/writer/artist (and/or: do you feel comfortable calling yourself a poet/writer/artist, what other titles or affiliations do you prefer/feel are more accurate)?

Born this way.

What's a "poet" (or "writer" or "artist") anyway? What do you see as your cultural and social role (in the literary / artistic / creative community and beyond)?

I think one thing poets are interested in the most is order, as in reason. It's sorta like when someone says something and you "look" for the joke you could make. There is a hidden order or reason underlying complicated things and sometimes it's really easy and obvious, often it's negative, but the upside is that understanding something better is necessarily a form of relief. People always say that about mathematics. Poets are sort of in the business of finding that exact order and reason. Comedians do the exact same thing. We all know why they're here. They're motivated, above all, by communication. But like I said that's just one thing.

Talk about the process or instinct to move these poems (or your work in general) as independent entities into a body of work. How and why did this happen? Have you had this intention for a while? What encouraged and/or confounded this (or a book, in general) coming together? Was it a struggle?

At a certain point I realized that poetry and science fiction as speculative endeavors have a lot in common, and putting LCHF together was about showing how that works for me. Making the distinction between a hybrid work and a mixed-genre work is—very crucially—of no interest to me, but I predict it as being a topic of conversation about the book, which is fine. That conversation has been happening for fifty years, at least, and I'm happy to perpetuate the attitude that stories - whether they're stories, about people, that look like stories, or poems about whatever poems are about (?) that look like poems - are more important than classification.

A book that I looked to again and again while assembling this book was *Buffalo Gals, Won't You Come Out At Night? And Other Animal Presences* by Ursula K. Le Guin, who I could talk about all day and all night. It's a novella backed with selected poems and stories that she put together scrupulously. It's different from my book in an important way because the poems and stories had already been in other books she'd published, but she chose them to accompany the novella in an effort, I think, to show her audience something specific about her work that maybe wasn't very obvious, but was obviously important to her. And the subtitle, *And Other Animal Presences*, is a coy and deft way of not saying what the book is or contains, of avoiding classifications. Again, I literally can't shut up about her, but the point is that I wanted to make a book sorta like that, but starting from scratch.

Did you envision this collection as a collection or understand your process as writing or making specifically around a theme while the poems themselves were being written / the work was being made? How or how not?

Once I started writing science fiction I knew what this book was going to be like. I definitely make and abandon lots of plans always. I actually am not so much a poet and science fiction writer as a person who takes a lot of notes and makes lists and forgets about them. Somewhere in there, though, I knew what I wanted the book to be about and how I wanted to work against that. It was my quaint little mass/energy equivalence.

What formal structures or other constrictive practices (if any) do you use in the creation of your work? Have certain teachers or instructive environments, or readings/writings/work of other creative people informed the way you work/write?

Obvious practices include, in the poems, the avoidance of periods and punctuation in general, which shapes the poems visually in a huge way, which come to think of it might not seem obvious. I don't use periods because I don't think poems or images ever really conclude, except that they do so who knows what in the world I'm saying when I say that. As far as the way I work and write goes, I definitely learned a lot—and continue to learn—from the essays of Theodore Roethke and UKL. Both are extremely, extremely technical writers who are very good at disguising that.

They are also both very intuitive writers, and there's a mystery there that I don't have much to say about.

As a science fiction writer I am, for better or worse, very fixated on the 60's and 70's, on the growing pains of pulp, and on when people first started to point out that SF was really important—and how those things led to where we are now. And sometimes I tell people that I use the science fiction short story as a poetic form, but that is, as UKL would say, a telling. I guess I would say that it's writers like Joanna Russ and Samuel R. Delaney and Stanislaw Lem that sit on my shoulder the most - only because I'm too new to the game to put what I've learned from Jeff VanderMeer and Ted Chiang—who are at the top of said game—into practice. Yet. Which is not to say that the latter are somehow writing some sort of more advanced SF than the former—it's just to say that so far I have written from what I've read and that tends to be older things. I definitely don't consider my science fiction to be contemporary or old-fashioned, either. I don't consider it to be anything because I don't actually know what it is at all.

Speaking of monikers, what does your title represent? How was it generated? Talk about the way you titled the book, and how your process of naming (individual pieces, sections, etc) influences you and/or colors your work specifically.

The lost city hydrothermal field is a geological feature of the Atlantic Ocean. It is a cluster of methane and hydrogen vents which are sometimes called "chimneys." I became attracted to this phrase because it superimposes certain human, architectural, and folkloric narratives onto a geophysical one. Carl Sagan might've called this a chauvinist act; today it might be called an anthropocentric act. I associate this particular type of act with a phenomenon in psychology called pareidolia, which is when the mind looks for and finds human faces and figures everywhere it looks. Sometimes the mind is wrong, as when it was thought that there was an earthwork on Mars created in the likeness of a human(oid) face. I see these acts and mistakes as being pretty central to a lot of dilemmas our civilizations face in the 21st century—and moving forward—as we learn that the human face and human presence in general is not everywhere.

As far as titles go in general: I have two answers to that. Somewhere in Witold Gombrowicz's notorious *Diary* he states that one names one's book as one names one's dog - to distinguish it from others. I took this to heart many years ago when I first encountered his very humorous and devastating work.

I was also, as a very young poet, urged to carefully and bombastically create titles - by a professor of mine at The New School named Sekou Sundiata. There is a poem in this book that addresses this issue head on, conveniently! Sekou was very captivated by placenames, specifically, and their power to evoke narrative tension, even if the word was seemingly meaningless. His famous example of that was always

Braintree, Massachusetts. This almost absurdist impulse still seems oddly out of character for him, but it's an impulse that carries over to creating a title no matter what it had to be (see his amazing poem "Mood For Love"). Make the poem work for it, he said. So I always try to, and I think of him every single time without exception. He is my pool of light.

What does this particular work represent to you
...as indicative of your method/creative practice?
...as indicative of your history?
...as indicative of your mission/intentions/hopes/plans?

OK breaking the third wall with this one. I do the work for nothing because that's my greatest reward.

What does this book DO (as much as what it says or contains)?

Against hyperobjects, human beings promise deluxe resistance. The truth is out there.

What would be the best possible outcome for this book? What might it do in the world, and how will its presence as an object facilitate your creative role in your community and beyond? What are your hopes for this book, and for your practice?

First of all I hope that this book makes the next book super hard to write. I know that already. That's for me. Also I want my friends to like it. I want Kesha to like it. Also I got lucky. And I wrote whatever the fuck I wanted to, and everyone deserves the same opportunity and license. Kurt Vonnegut said something about that. We out here. Find us. We're not alone. I hope someone I don't know at all finds this book and discovers something in it that I didn't know was there. And makes something out of it I could never predict in my wildest dreams.

Let's talk a little bit about the role of poetics and creative community in social activism, in particular in what I call "Civil Rights 2.0," which has remained immediately present all around us in the time leading up to this series' publication. I'd be curious to hear some thoughts on the challenges we face in speaking and publishing across lines of race, age, privilege, social/cultural background, and sexuality within the community, vs. the dangers of remaining and producing in isolated "silos."

This question is at the heart of the ethos of The Operating System, and it's the heartest to answer. In Harold Bloom's (bear with me) *The Flight To Lucifer*, a sequel to David Lindsay's *A Voyage To Arcturus* (by some definitions an early work of science fiction) (Bloom has disowned his first and only novel just as many people have disowned all of his work) there is a strange tower at the edge of a strange lake. A kind of silo. At first there doesn't seem to be an entrance to this tower. One word that comes to mind when I hear this question is marginalization. I'm not sure I have accomplished anything, or have done anything. I didn't do anything because process and the work that emerges from process does not (always) happen that way, although it sometimes does; sometimes it often does, depending on how you look and where you look. A willingness to look is what I'm talking about. And recognizing that process exists, to paraphrase the Vulcans, as an infinite diversity in infinite combinations. And this entanglement of human stories exempts no one. Everyone is responsible. And everyone, contrary to what I said before, is everywhere. My tiny piece of the puzzle is a little silo, a word worth reclaiming; they are ubiquitous; we consist of them. There's a silo of sorts on the cover of this book. It's a defunct particle accelerator. It has been superimposed over a strange landscape. It has a troubled, complicated history. One we might never really understand. We all have histories like that. Kazuo Ishigoru said something like that. The only way we will ever learn from such things is to place them—squarely, securely, and with accountability - in the record.

PMG
Brooklyn NY
August 12th, 2017

PETER MILNE GREINER is a poet and science fiction writer. His work has appeared in *Motherboard, Fence, Dark Mountain, SciArt Magazine, Big Echo: Critical Science Fiction, Berfrois, Forklift Ohio,* and elsewhere. *Lost City Hydrothermal Field* is his first full-length collection. He lives in Brooklyn and works at a hotel.

A NOTE ABOUT THIS VOLUME
AND GRATITUDE TO ITS AUTHOR

Peter Milne Greiner is an exceptional writer, thinker, and human being, and I have faith that with this volume his articulate, wry, timely observations and wholly original use of language will find the audience it so deeply deserves.

But also, over the last years PMG has become an integral part of this evolving thing called The Operating System -- a true comrade in what can be at times an infuriating and exhausting, thankless process, giving more of himself and his hours than I can count or fully comprehend.

I felt it would be remiss, given the OS's commitment to the archive, to not have this enter the archive alongside it -- PMG is a humble person, not one to shout his gifts or achievements from the rooftops or expect anything in return...so here I am, happy to be the loudmouth, embarassing him I'm sure.

We exist in a system where cronyism is a huge problem, and so I'll speak to that too: in no way shape or form does this book exist as a kickback for labor. In fact, I came to know Peter because I was so astounded by his work at a reading circa 2011 that I approached him after the show to convince him to submit it to a new arts and literature magazine, *Exit Strata* -- the magazine which would morph into The Operating System not long after. Much to my delight he agreed, and my respect for him and his work continued to grow.

Part of that respect comes from an understanding of community. From day one, this is a person who has been willing not only to *attend* community, as an observer / consumer, but someone who has understood that this thing we are growing only has a "we" if you show up, offer of yourself in exchange, and participate not only in elements that directly serve you.

When I read this book (which I will do many more times) I am astounded again and again by the rich, nuanced, informed, humane intelligence of this person I am so lucky to call collaborator and friend. Thank you for all you have done for The OS, for me -- and for everyone, with these pages.

- LDJ

The Operating System uses the language "print document" to differentiate from the book-object as part of our mission to distinguish the act of documentation-in-book-FORM from the act of publishing as a backwards facing replication of the book's agentive *role* as it may have appeared the last several centuries of its history. Ultimately, I approach the book as TECHNOLOGY: one of a variety of printed documents (in this case bound) that humans have invented and in turn used to archive and disseminate ideas, beliefs, stories, and other evidence of production.

Ownership and use of printing presses and access to (or restriction of printed materials) has long been a site of struggle, related in many ways to revolutionary activity and the fight for civil rights and free speech all over the world. While (in many countries) the contemporary quotidian landscape has indeed drastically shifted in its access to platforms for sharing information and in the widespread ability to "publish" digitally, even with extremely limited resources, the importance of publication on physical media has not diminished. In fact, this may be the most critical time in recent history for activist groups, artists, and others to insist upon learning, establishing, and encouraging personal and community documentation practices. Hear me out.

With The OS's print endeavors I wanted to open up a conversation about this: the ultimately radical, transgressive act of creating PRINT /DOCUMENTATION in the digital age. It's a question of the archive, and of history: who gets to tell the story, and what evidence of our life, our behaviors, our experiences are we leaving behind? We can know little to nothing about the future into which we're leaving an unprecedentedly digital document trail — but we can be assured that publications, government agencies, museums, schools, and other institutional powers that be will continue to leave BOTH a digital and print version of their production for the official record. Will we?

As a (rogue) anthropologist and long time academic, I can easily pull up many accounts about how lives, behaviors, experiences — how THE STORY of a time or place — was pieced together using the deep study of correspondence, notebooks, and other physical documents which are no longer the norm in many lives and practices. As we move our creative behaviors towards digital note taking, and even audio and video, what can we predict about future technology that is in any way assuring that our stories will be accurately told – or told at all? How will we leave these things for the record?

In these documents we say:
WE WERE HERE, WE EXISTED, WE HAVE A DIFFERENT STORY

- Lynne DeSilva-Johnson, Founder/Managing Editor,
THE OPERATING SYSTEM, Brooklyn NY 2017

TITLES IN THE PRINT: DOCUMENT COLLECTION

An Absence So Great and Spontaneous It Is Evidence of Light - Anne Gorrick [2018]
Chlorosis - Michael Flatt and Derrick Mund [2018]
Sussuros a Mi Padre - Erick Sáenz [2018]
Sharing Plastic - Blake Nemec [2018]
The Book of Sounds - Mehdi Navid (Farsi dual language, trans. Tina Rahimi) [2018]
In Corpore Sano : Creative Practice and the Challenged Body
[Anthology, 2018] Lynne DeSilva-Johnson and Jay Besemer, co-editors
Abandoners - Lesley Ann Wheeler [2018]
Jazzercise is a Language - Gabriel Ojeda-Sague [2018]
Death is a Festival - Anis Shivani [2018]
Return Trip / Viaje Al Regreso; Dual Language Edition -
Israel Dominguez,(trans. Margaret Randall) [2018]
Born Again - Ivy Johnson [2018]
Singing for Nothing - Wally Swist [2018]
The Unspoken - Bob Holman [2018]

One More Revolution - Andrea Mazzariello [2017]
Fugue State Beach - Filip Marinovich [2017]
Lost City Hydrothermal Field - Peter Milne Greiner [2017]
The Book of Everyday Instruction - Chloe Bass [2017]
An Exercise in Necromancy - Patrick Roche [Bowery Poetry Imprint, 2017]
Love, Robot - Margaret Rhee[2017]
La Comandante Maya - Rita Valdivia (dual language, trans. Margaret Randall) [2017]
The Furies - William Considine [2017]
Nothing Is Wasted - Shabnam Piryaei [2017]
Mary of the Seas - Joanna C. Valente [2017]
Secret-Telling Bones - Jessica Tyner Mehta [2017]
CHAPBOOK SERIES 2017 : INCANTATIONS
featuring original cover art by Barbara Byers
sp. - Susan Charkes; Radio Poems - Jeffrey Cyphers Wright; Fixing a Witch/Hexing the
Stitch - Jacklyn Janeksela; cosmos a personal voyage by carl sagan ann druyan steven
sotor and me - Connie Mae Oliver
Flower World Variations, Expanded Edition/Reissue - Jerome
Rothenberg and Harold Cohen [2017]
What the Werewolf Told Them / Lo Que Les Dijo El Licantropo -
Chely Lima (trans. Margaret Randall) [2017]
The Color She Gave Gravity - Stephanie Heit [2017]
The Science of Things Familiar - Johnny Damm [Graphic Hybrid, 2017]
agon - Judith Goldman [2017]
To Have Been There Then / Estar Alli Entonces - Gregory Randall
(trans. Margaret Randall) [2017]

Instructions Within - Ashraf Fayadh [2016]
Arabic-English dual language edition; Mona Kareem, translator
Let it Die Hungry - Caits Meissner [2016]
A GUN SHOW - Adam Sliwinski and Lynne DeSilva-Johnson;
So Percussion in Performance with Ain Gordon and Emily Johnson [2016]
Everybody's Automat [2016] - Mark Gurarie
How to Survive the Coming Collapse of Civilization [2016] - Sparrow
CHAPBOOK SERIES 2016: OF SOUND MIND
*featuring the quilt drawings of Daphne Taylor
Improper Maps - Alex Crowley; While Listening - Alaina Ferris;
Chords - Peter Longofono; Any Seam or Needlework - Stanford Cheung

TEN FOUR - Poems, Translations, Variations [2015]- Jerome Rothenberg, Ariel
Resnikoff, Mikhl Likht
MARILYN [2015] - Amanda Ngoho Reavey
CHAPBOOK SERIES 2015: OF SYSTEMS OF
*featuring original cover art by Emma Steinkraus
Cyclorama - Davy Knittle; The Sensitive Boy Slumber Party Manifesto
- Joseph Cuillier; Neptune Court - Anton Yakovlev; Schema - Anurak Saelow
SAY/MIRROR [2015; 2nd edition 2016] - JP HOWARD
Moons Of Jupiter/Tales From The Schminke Tub [plays, 2014] - Steve Danziger

CHAPBOOK SERIES 2014: BY HAND
Pull, A Ballad - Maryam Parhizkar; Can You See that Sound - Jeff Musillo
Executive Producer Chris Carter - Peter Milne Greiner;
Spooky Action at a Distance - Gregory Crosby;

CHAPBOOK SERIES 2013: WOODBLOCK
*featuring original prints from Kevin William Reed
Strange Coherence - Bill Considine; The Sword of Things - Tony Hoffman;
Talk About Man Proof - Lancelot Runge / John Kropa; An Admission as a Warning
Against the Value of Our Conclusions -Alexis Quinlan

DOC U MENT
/däkyəmənt/

First meant "instruction" or "evidence," whether written or not.

noun - a piece of written, printed, or electronic matter that provides
information or evidence or that serves as an official record
verb - record (something) in written, photographic, or other form
synonyms - paper - deed - record - writing - act - instrument

[*Middle English, precept, from Old French, from Latin documentum,
example, proof, from docre, to teach; see dek- in Indo-European roots.*]

Who is responsible for the manufacture of value?

Based on what supercilious ontology have we landed in a space where we vie against other
creative people in vain pursuit of the fleeting credibilities of the scarcity economy,
rather than freely collaborating and sharing openly with each other
in ecstatic celebration of MAKING?

While we understand and acknowledge the economic pressures and fear-mongering
that threatens to dominate and crush the creative impulse,
we also believe that ***now more than ever
we have the tools to relinquish agency via cooperative means,***
fueled by the fires of the Open Source Movement.

**Looking out across the invisible vistas of that rhizomatic parallel country
we can begin to see our community beyond constraints,
in the place where intention meets
resilient, proactive, collaborative organization.**

Here is a document born of that belief, sown purely of imagination and will.
When we document we assert.
We print to make real, to reify our being there.
When we do so with mindful intention to address our process,
to open our work to others, to create beauty in words in space,
to respect and acknowledge the strength of the page we now hold physical,
a thing in our hand… we remind ourselves that, like Dorothy:
we had the power all along, my dears.

THE PRINT! DOCUMENT SERIES
is a project of
the trouble with bartleby
in collaboration with
the operating system